SALVATION
(NYC DOMS)

JANE HENRY

SALVATION

NYC DOMS

By: Jane Henry

Chapter One

"Doubt thou the stars are fire, Doubt that the sun doth move. Doubt truth to be a liar, But never doubt I love." ~ *William Shakespeare,* Hamlet

Chandra

I shiver when I enter the club, and I'm not sure if it's the biting cold or fear that makes me tremble.

I shouldn't be here. I don't belong.

I considered some type of disguise coming here, but then I realized that anyone who would recognize me would be just as guilty as I am.

There's a bouncer at the door, and a particularly strong gust of wind picks up just as he lets me in. I brace against the blast of cold, and he reaches for me, shielding me against the bitter blast of air and shutting the large black door behind me. It bangs with an audible click that makes me jump. Already, I'm out of my element. Men don't touch me without permission.

But this is a BDSM club, and apparently no one plays by my rulebook. The one I was raised with. If I didn't want someone to touch me, I wouldn't be here.

"Name?" The man asks. He's wearing a black t-shirt stretched tight over his muscled chest, stands well over six feet, and looks severe with a neatly-trimmed goatee and shaved head. He's staring at a huge clipboard in his hand.

I blink and stare at him. *Shit.* I didn't know I was supposed to give my name.

He looks up at me and raises a brow when a beat passes. I'm frozen. I can't tell him who I am. And where the hell is Marla? My strategy to meet up with her definitely could've been improved.

But then again, she doesn't know I don't want anyone to know who I am.

"Chandra," I whisper, hoping that's enough. Does he need my last name, too? Because then I'm screwed. But he gives me a curious look, glances back down at his clipboard, and nods.

"Marla's guest?" he asks.

At that moment, I hear a familiar squeal. "Chandra! You did it, girl! Come on in!"

Marla makes her way to me and the bouncer. "Master Geoffrey, this is my new employee. Her name is Chandra." I smile at him and he shakes my hand, but then the door opens again, and two more people come in behind us. Marla grabs my hand and pulls me past the entryway door. There's an office and what looks like a sitting room of sorts.

"If you come here with your dom, you can discuss your limits and things like that in this room," Marla says.

My dom? I don't have a dom.

"We have contracts and stuff like that. Over there is Master Tobias' office." She waves across the room to an open doorway, where a man sits at a desk typing on a computer. "He's awesome, and you'll love his wife Diana. In fact, you're gonna love a lot of the people here," she says with warmth. "I do."

I nod dumbly when a couple walks through the door that leads to the club. I expected all leather and latex, but they're dressed pretty normally. When they open a door from the room I'm in now, I hear music and voices, and I freeze. Once I step foot in there, there's no going back. This is it.

But I can't turn back now. I've been living and breathing everything I could get my hands on about the BDSM lifestyle for a full year, and I'm so ready to see what this is like.

"Let's go," Marla says, taking me by the hand and giving me a tug. She's the least bashful person I know, and right now, I'm so grateful for that.

"There's a bar," she says. "Drinks are limited for safety reasons, but we can get you a good, stiff drink to start."

I don't tell her that I have literally never in my life touched alcohol. But tonight is a night of firsts.

"Sure," I say quietly. She leads me to the bar.

I'm trying to take in all the details, but it's a little overwhelming, and I'm starting to feel that my too-tight black dress that I was so proud of for hitting my badass radar is really way too tame for a place like this. A woman walks past me wearing what looks like a purple leotard, complete with a tail and kitty ears. I must look wide-eyed and shocked, because Marla laughs and hands me a pretty pink drink. I take a sip. It's delicious.

"Drink, honey," she says. "You'll be fine."

"Got a friend with you tonight, Marla?" asks the man at the bar. He's got a southern drawl and looks like he's about my age, with sandy-brown hair and light brown eyes. He's attractive, and seems sweet, so I take his hand and shake it.

"Chandra," I tell him.

He smiles, revealing dimples on either side of his mouth. "Travis. Pleased to meet you, Chandra." I say something barely coherent, but fortunately he's already moving on to the the next person waiting for a drink. My mind is racing. This man's a dom? Is he a sadist, too? Does he like to tie people up? Inflict pain? Does he have rules? I take another long pull from my drink.

I haven't eaten all day, I've been so nervous about coming here tonight, and I'm not so sure it's a smart idea having my first-ever alcoholic drink on an empty stomach. The room feels hot and stuffy, and my head is a little wobbly. I watch Travis fill other girls' drinks and feel disappointed. He looked easy to talk to. And men are rarely easy to talk to.

Marla's perched up on the stool next to me,

sipping her drink. "So over there we've got pool tables for everyone to just mingle. This is sort of the meet-and-greet area."

"Mhm." I take another gulp of my drink.

"And beyond that area…" her voice trails off. I watch as couples and single people make their way to a hallway. Someone screams, and I nearly drop my glass. I look with wide eyes at Marla. She smiles and nods.

"The dungeon, honey. That's where the real action takes place."

"It's not in a basement?" I ask curiously. I had visions of the dungeon being built with bricks, complete with metal handcuffs and no lighting whatsoever.

Marla smiles. "Not in this club, no. It's just what we call it."

I finish my drink, plunk it on the counter, and turn to her. Liquid courage, they say. Already, I know why. "Take me?"

She finishes her drink, too, and places it on the bar. "Absolutely."

The room spins, and my head feels light. But I like this. I feel braver. Maybe even more powerful. I've gotten brave enough to come to my first BDSM club, and I'm not just here to mingle. Tonight, I want to see what this is like.

A couple jostles past me, and I lose my footing, but Marla quickly rights me. Still, it makes me feel like I'm on a merry-go-round. I'm definitely woozy, and not sure I like this feeling very much. Why do people do this on a regular basis? I like being in control of myself, and this is stupid.

I follow her past the crowd to the dungeon, excitement building.

"Down here are the private rooms for long-term members," she says. "They're color-coordinated, and long-term members keep their things here. It's like a second home."

"Do you have one?" I ask, shouting to be heard above the noise of the crowd.

"I could," she says thoughtfully, and her eyes grow a little pained. "I don't have a need for one, though."

Marla's single. I nod. But it's at that very moment, just before I step into the dungeon, that I hear a voice that makes my whole body seize. I know that voice.

"Not here," he says. "Take that somewhere else." It's calm but stern and brooks no argument. I look around me to see where the voice is coming from, but there are too many people here.

It's got to be in my head. Some people sound like others, and I've just had a drink. Plus, I'm all keyed up. There's no way that's *his* voice.

But I'd know that voice anywhere. It's the voice I conjure up when I go to sleep at night, to chase my demons away so I can rest. The voice branded into my memory like names carved in stone, lasting and irrevocable. In my mind, I tell myself it can't be him. There's no way. But in that moment, I'm no longer an anonymous woman who's having a little fun at a BDSM club. I'm the girl who made terrible decisions she lived to regret. All of it comes rushing back to me in a flood of memories I can't ignore, and I try to push it all away, but I'm frozen in place.

"Chandra?" Marla's looking at me with concern, her head tipped to the side. She reaches a hand to my elbow. "Honey, if this is too much, that's okay. We don't have to go in here tonight."

"No," I say, shaking my head. I need to exorcise my past from my memory and know I came here and didn't cave. I swallow hard and take a deep, cleansing breath. "Let's go."

She nods, and her eyes sparkle at me. "Let's go."

When I step foot in the dungeon, I feel something in me shift. I expected to be shocked. And maybe a part of me is, a little. There are some couples wearing outfits that range from outlandish to scandalous, men and women and people wearing masks for anonymity. There are all sorts of activities going on, but it doesn't shock me. Maybe it's the drink or maybe it's because I was so freaked out by hearing the voice that yanked me back to my youth, but I'm excited. My whole body thrums with nervous, eager anticipation.

"Over there is the Saint Andrew's Cross," Marla says, pointing to crossed beams against a wall. No one's on there yet, but I have read enough to know how that works. "We have spanking benches and horses," she says, gesturing to a setup of sturdy-looking equipment. "We have some implements couples can use over clothing, but private implements only for bare skin."

I shiver. I want someone to use an implement on *my* bare skin.

There are couples sitting on loveseats. I blink at first in surprise, and it takes me a minute to realize that some of them are actually doing sexual things. Right here. In front of *everyone*. One man's feeling a girl up, tweaking her bare nipples right over the edge of a too-short top. Her head's thrown back, lips parted. I watch as he bends his head down and flicks his tongue over a nipple. My own body heats with arousal. *Oh my God.*

"I thought you said there were private rooms," I say to Marla in a choked voice.

She grins. "For long-term members only," she says. "And also? Not everyone's here for private play."

I look back at the couple. He's rubbing between her legs while he suckles at her breasts. She's writhing against his hand. I watch in rapt fascination. She's going to climax. Right here. Clothed, and in front of everyone in this room. My own body heats as he moves faster and faster. Is it possible to climax without even being touched? Because this man must be a magician. I'm ready to fly.

I tear my eyes away.

I hear someone speaking right near me.

"That's enough, little one." I look to see where this voice comes from. There's an older man with dark hair and eyes crossing his arms on his chest. He's looking reproachfully at a small blonde woman wearing kitty ears. "Behave yourself," he says.

What happens if she doesn't? My pulse thunders. I've read enough books to know exactly what happens in the world of fiction. What happens here? I watch as she shakes her head with a pout befitting a little girl.

Oh my God. She told him no?

He shakes his head with regret and takes her by the arm. "I warned you," he says. He's marching her over to one of the spanking benches but there's a gleam in his eyes like he hoped she'd disobey. On the way, he grabs the varnished wooden handle of a paddle. I can't breathe or speak, but only watch. He's going to punish her.

I catch a glimpse of her face. She's grinning.

I'd be beet red. But at the same time… I want to know what it feels like.

He bends her over the bench, expertly fastens her restraints, then stands behind her wielding the paddle. Placing one hand on her lower back, he lifts his right hand and brings it slamming down on the woman's clothed ass. She squeals, and he says something in her ear, then brings the paddle down again and again. Every time the wood strikes, blood thunders in my ears. My pussy clenches. I'm so wet, my panties feel damp.

I'm so primed for this.

"Chandra?" Marla's next to me. She's been talking to me, but I've been too busy getting turned on watching the girl get paddled.

"Yes?" I croak.

"This is my friend Viktor," she says. He's shorter than the guy at the door but broad and stern-looking the way I imagined a dom would be, and I'm a little intimidated.

"Hi," I say. I swallow and must look like a total

idiot, because I let my eyes go all wide so he doesn't know I'm aroused by the scene in front of me. It must be a funny thing being introduced to a man when you're aroused, and I wonder if it affects my vision, because this man is beautiful and the whole tall, dark, and handsome thing isn't normally my thing.

Then I notice the way he's looking at Marla. He stands just a little too close and his eyes warm when she introduces us.

"Pleased to meet you," he says. He's got a barely-detectable accent that makes him seem even sterner. God, I need another drink.

"Join me tonight?" he says to Marla. She blinks at him and her cheeks pink.

"Well," she says. "I actually need to stay with Chandra. It's her first time here, and I don't want to leave her."

He nods. "Fair enough."

But I see the way he looks at her, and I know how desperate Marla's been for someone to pay attention to her. She's been a member here since they opened, and the other guys that she knows are all friends. They think of her as a sister, not a potential sub, and though she loves the camaraderie and occasional scene, it isn't what she wants. I'd be a crappy friend to hold her back.

"Go," I tell her. "I'm actually just going to get another drink and then just come back and watch. You know. Like a fly on the wall. A voyeur?" I chatter on like someone's wound my tongue up and let it go. "A fly voyeur on the wall." *Dear God, someone stopper my mouth.*

She blinks. "You sure you need another drink?"

"Oh, so very, very sure."

Viktor chuckles, but takes Marla by the hand. "Be my sub tonight?" he asks.

She looks at me and blinks, then looks back to him.

"Do it," I tell her.

"Wait for me in the foyer," Viktor says in his heavily accented voice. "If we're scening tonight, we'll have ground rules. I have a quick phone call to make, then we talk."

My heartbeat accelerates. This is it! This is what she wanted, and I'm simultaneously consumed with jealousy and excitement for my friend.

"Have fun, you two," I say, turning away from her and heading back to the bar.

"Text me," she says, raising her voice. "If anything goes wrong at all, and you need to—"

But her voice fades as Viktor gives her a playful slap on the bottom. She faces him, he whispers something in her ear, and she nods, then goes beet red

I look away. My heart twists and my throat burns. There's a little tingle in my nose. What the hell is wrong with me? I'm not sad that she's with him. I'm just… jealous?

As I walk alone to the bar, I know, I wouldn't have made a different choice. I don't need a babysitter here. I'm only here to observe, and there is *no way* I'm participating in anything tonight. Like, at all. But this is hard for me. I grew

JANE HENRY

up in a home where I wasn't even allowed to date. My parents arranged my marriage like their parents did, and even though I bailed on that, a part of me still fears disapproval. If they knew I was here tonight, they'd disown me.

If they knew a lot of things, they'd disown me.

I make my way to the bar. I need a drink *stat.*

"Hey," Travis says. He's a friendly guy, and really kinda cute, though he looks pretty young, and that feels more like he's my brother than a potential... well, anything. Dom. Boyfriend. Guy I kiss who buys me a drink. I've never been one who's attracted to men my age, and I'm not now.

"Marla took off?" he asks. He wipes his hands on a towel. I can't help but glance at his ring finger. He doesn't wear a ring, but he's got to be in his early twenties or so, and bartenders flirt even if they're dating someone. He's kind, though, and that's always been my weakness.

"Well, she's spending the night with a guy," I say, and then realize that sounds like my friend is whoring herself out. "I mean—well. Okay, so I don't really know how it works here?" I grimace. God, I should just shut up right now. "But there's a guy named Viktor and he wanted to, um... what's the word... scene with her. So they're going to go... I don't know, write up a contract or something?" I've been into this for *how* long and now I sound like a total newbie? God!

His eyes crinkle around the edges and he smiles at me. "Is that right? Seems like Marla's in need of scenin' good and hard."

"Most of us are in need of scening good and

12

hard," I say before I can stop myself. My hand flies to my mouth and I look at him with wide eyes.

And just like that, the insane arousal that started when I saw the scene in the dungeon ignites. Travis grins.

"Is that right?" he asks in his panty-melting drawl.

Hell. Maybe he *is* cute.

I shouldn't have come here. I'm way too sex-deprived and needy. I need to get out of here.

"That's right," I squeak. I grab a handful of the nuts in the little bowl on the counter, and pop some in my mouth so I don't say anything stupid. My mind starts playing tricks on me. Travis bending me over the bar and showing me exactly what "scenin' good and hard" looks like. I imagine he reaches for his belt buckle, those golden-brown eyes growing stern and corrective.

Someone lifts their hand across the bar and Travis shoots me a parting wink, then goes to fill the order. I barely restrain myself from burying my head in my hands.

"Buy you a drink?" someone to my right asks.

I look over and there are three men sitting there that look like they could be brothers with Viktor. Maybe they are. Or cousins or something.

"Sorry?" I ask.

"You look like you need a drink," the younger one says. "First time here?"

I nod dumbly. He waves down Travis. "What's your drink?" he asks me.

I shrug like a dumbass.

"Whiskey sour's what Marla gave you." Travis looks disapprovingly at me, and gives me the drink, but shoots the guys next to me a warning look. Is it my imagination? Is he jealous?

I hear someone laughing so loudly behind me, it catches my attention, and I quickly turn and look. There's a crowd of people dressed up in all black, over by the pool tables. I can't quite tell what they're doing, but they're having so much fun. I'm a little jealous, and I know then that I want to be a part of this place. I want to fit in. Have friends that know me and welcome me when I come. And hell, I want to scene.

"What brings you here?" the man next to me asks. He's got a similar accent to Viktor. Russian? He pushes my drink to me, and I take it gratefully.

"Thank you," I say. I gulp it like I'm dying of thirst. The voice I heard plays in my mind, and I need to get it to stop. I'm not that girl anymore, and I don't act like her.

"Whoa, now," the man says, holding his hand palm down. "Take it easy there. Travis is known for his good, strong drinks."

My head is feeling woozy again and my mouth a little thick. "Is he known for good, strong anything else?" I ask.

Oh my God. Did I just say that out loud? The men just laugh, though. I drink until ice hits my lips. Marla's with her man. After tonight, I may never be brave enough to return. Tonight, I'm living it up.

Chapter Two

Axle

It's my first night as dungeon monitor at Club Verge and there's a blizzard warning. It's twenty-two degrees in New York City, but that doesn't stop the kinksters. They're a dedicated crowd, not put off by things like natural disasters, and anyway, the forecaster who called tonight's blizzard has a history of doomsday warnings that amount to shit, so people have stopped listening to him. But when Zack, my friend and fellow member of Club Verge, comes in, he comes straight to me.

"Snow's already started, Axle," he says, shaking his head as he scans the crowd. I'm almost used to people calling me *Axle*. It isn't my real name, but I'm not the person I used to be, so I keep assuming my new identity.

"Yeah. I noticed. You looking for Beatrice?" I

ask. His wife Beatrice arrived here earlier with her friend Diana. Club owner Tobias, Diana's husband, escorted them both in, and the two of them were having drinks at the bar.

"Yeah, I found her. Just sayin', that weather isn't looking good," Zack says.

"Great," I mutter. It'll be easy enough to hail a cab and head home when I need to, but I won't leave until I know every single person here has gone home safely. Ah, well. I don't have to work at the shop tomorrow, which is why I took this shift to begin with.

Still, it's gonna be a long night.

"I'll go see if Tobias is closing early," I say. "Keep an eye on things here for me?"

Zack nods, scanning the small crowd and he smirks. "Seems like a rowdy bunch but I'll do my best."

As I go to exit the dungeon, Beatrice and Diana walk in. Beatrice is tiny with crazy blonde hair pulled up in a messy bun. Diana, tall and graceful with a mane of curls that cascades down her back, grins at me. She's part club-owner with her husband Tobias, and knows this is my first night as DM.

"Looks like it's about to get rowdier," I quip, earning me a playful punch from Beatrice and an eye-roll from Diana. Zack takes Beatrice's little clenched fist and *tsks* at her.

"What do you guys think of the weather?" Diana asks, sobering. She crosses her arms on her chest and looks around the room.

"Not sure," I say. "I was just going to see what Tobias thought."

"I have a say, too, you know," she says playfully, but there's a fire in her eyes. She just wants to remind me that yes, her husband is owner of the club, but she is, too, and it might be good to check my traditionalist views at the door.

"I know," I say. "But you're not sitting in the office. Promise, I'm just being lazy, not a chauvinist."

She grins. "I know."

"So what do you think?" I ask her.

She frowns. "It's not looking good. It's hard to make the call, though, since tonight's packed to capacity, and the weather could amount to nothing." Her eyes twinkle. "You know what? Why don't you see what Tobias thinks."

"You are such a brat," Beatrice says. "And filled to capacity? Looks like we just got a little busier," Beatrice says. As if on cue, a large crowd of people enters the dungeon at once. I raise a brow to Beatrice who merely shrugs.

"Maybe a movie got out or something," she mutters. Soon, the dungeon is filled with couples and singles, laughing and mingling, and the large room comes to life. The St. Andrew's Cross in the corner is quickly occupied, as well as several of the spanking benches we have. Verge is comfortably outfitted with some of the finest, well-made BDSM accoutrements, and the classy, cozy atmosphere of Verge typically draws large crowds. We're a members-only club, though, so I expect there's been some kind of a meet-up planned for tonight, and this crowd isn't letting a potential snow storm ruin their fun.

"Yeah, check with Tobias," Diana says, then shrugs. "No big deal, though, guys. We all have private rooms, so if it gets bad we can stay here." Verge has a series of color-coded private rooms long-term members have access to, complete with beds and bathrooms and a variety of tools anyone spending the night might use. My room, the crimson room, is the one at the far end of the hall. Sound-proof and utterly private, I consider it my sanctuary when I want to get to know a submissive a little better.

Theoretically. It's been a long, long time since I've taken anyone there privately.

On my way to Tobias's office, I hear someone call my name.

"Axle!"

I turn to find my friend Marla, another long-term member, the resident bookstore owner. She and I have become good friends over the years, as I spend as much of my free time in Books and Cups, her store, as I do at Club Verge.

"Finally took your advice and hired help," she says, smiling. Marla's a petite woman with nondescript brown hair, freckled cheeks, and right now it's all I can do to refrain from giving her pert nose a little twist. She's adorable, but I know that would insult her. There was a time when we thought we could be a couple. It became pretty clear we were not dom/sub material, and we cooled things off to friendship-level, but she hates when anyone thinks she's cute.

"Good—for you," I say haltingly. I almost call her *good girl*, but that's a term for a sub, not a friend. "Tell me about it?"

"I have good news," she says. "I put in ad online, and pretty quickly found someone willing to take me up on it. You know I really need help stocking the shelves and manning the coffee shop."

Her store, not too far from Verge, has risen in popularity ever since the local paper did an interview with her. Not only is she known for having the best lemon cake and coffee in NYC, she stocks the most extensive collection of romance novels, particularly those with a decidedly kinky flair. It's partly why I love her store.

"So I'm pretty excited for her to start. Chandra has been training with me the past week, and she starts tomorrow."

I ignore the clench in my gut at the name *Chandra.*

No.

I knew a Chandra once, but she's nothing more than a ghost, someone I left behind in my old life. I shove the memories that threaten to surface away, out of my mind, focusing myself on the present. But as hard as I try, I can't banish the memory of smooth, dark skin, deep brown eyes alight looking at me from beneath lowered lashes. I can still hear her voice. Feel her touch. Taste her mouth.

With considerable effort, I push her out of my mind.

That was then. This is now.

It's just a name. A name that belongs to

another woman, not the shadow of a memory that makes me shiver like cold, dead leaves in a vacant park.

"Nice," I say with a distracted nod, my voice tighter than I intend. "I look forward to meeting her."

"Might be sooner than later," she says in a singsong voice.

I look at her curiously. "Oh?"

Marla's eyes twinkle. "Yeah. It seems my penchant for kinky romance hasn't gone unnoticed."

"Definitely not," I say with a chuckle. "So you not only recruited a new barista-slash book fiend, you recruited a new member for Verge."

"Yup," she says with unmistakable pride. "Gotta go. Later!" She heads to the lobby.

I shake my head and take my leave, heading to Tobias's office. Still, I can't help but wonder who the new girl is. I'm one of the few dominants here at Verge with no romantic attachments. I watch them come and I watch them go, but no one stirs anything in me. My purpose here is twofold: to meet a need of mine, and to pay for the sins I've committed. To offer to others what they need. It's why I was happy to take on a role of dungeon monitor, give guidance and instruction to those who seek it, even if only temporarily. Though my job as dominant is rewarding, my goal to exercise power and measured pain when necessary, to wield temporary authority with patience and strength, I also seek meekness.

To whom much has been given, much is expected.

The biblical refrain of my youth, a memory from a lifetime ago—no doubt brought back by the memory of Chandra—makes me smile to myself. Yes. A dominant wields power. Cherishes trust. And with that gift comes responsibility.

None of the subs who scene with me mean anything to me, though. None warm my bed at night. None of them ever will. I don't even know many of their names beyond the names they use when scening.

I knock on the doorframe of Tobias's office. His door is never closed, but I don't like to go in unannounced.

"Axle." Tobias doesn't look up from the computer but nods to the chair in front of his desk. "How's your first night going?"

"Good," I say, taking my seat in front of him. "I just wanted to talk to you about the weather forecast."

He looks up from his computer then and looks out the window behind him as if he's just noticed it's winter. "Sorry, man. I've been totally immersed in these new applications." He takes his job as club owner seriously.

"They're saying potential blizzard, Tobias. The snow's already coming down."

Tobias frowns. "We have new members coming tonight. I'd hate to shut the doors so soon, especially when the forecast has been total shit lately. I've closed these doors four times in the past month due to the forecast, only to have not a single flake fly before daybreak."

It's a hard call to make. And it isn't like a

school where children are coming, either. This is an adults-only club, so anyone who arrives comes here of their own volition.

He looks to me. "Would you close?"

I respect that he asks advice. He's got more responsibility on his shoulders than literally anyone else here, yet he asks me my opinion. I think about it, shaking my head. "Nah. I wouldn't close. If the winds pick up, then we can close. These are all adults. If they're worried about the forecast, they can stay home."

"Agreed," he says. "Thanks, man."

His gaze flickers back to the screen. I get it. He doesn't want to be impolite and dismiss me, but he has shit to do.

I stand. "Thanks, man. So there are lots of new members?" I ask, on my way to the door.

He nods, eyes back on the screen. "Couple of dozen. Mostly word of mouth."

Verge is growing and has been since they opened its doors. It's rare to find a place as classy as Verge in a place like NYC, where the population exceeds some Third World countries. BDSM clubs are aplenty. Trying to find one like Verge is another story. The growing membership is partly why Tobias hired me on as dungeon monitor, to protect the integrity of his club.

As I make my way back to the bar area, I can hear the wind picking up outside, whistling in the night like a scream. I shiver, and nearly collide into Diana.

"Sorry, you okay?" I ask, steadying her.

Her eyes are wide, but she takes a deep

breath. "I'm okay. But I need to go. The babysitter just called and Chad fell. Gotta take him to the hospital, and he's freaking out." Her son, and Tobias's step-son Chad, has special needs. It's rare that she gets called out like this but it's not unheard of.

"Okay," I say calmly, recognizing the need to stay in control for her. "Where's Beatrice?"

Diana releases a shuddering breath. "Bea and Zack went to their private room, and I don't want to interrupt them."

I nod. "I'll walk with you to Tobias. C'mon." She nods thankfully, and we walk back together to Tobias's office. Diana explains the problem, and Tobias listens patiently.

"You're the one who can calm him down best," Diana says, pleadingly. I stand to leave, but Tobias calls out to me before I leave.

"You staying here tonight, you said, Axle?"

"Yeah, man."

"Keep an eye on things so I can get my girl home?" He gets to his feet. "Zack's here for now, and Brax is, too. Call if you need them."

"Of course," I tell him. "I've got this."

He gives me a chin lift and stands, shutting down his computer. "Thanks man," he says. He takes Diana's hand and he pulls her close. It tugs at my heart a little, but I dismiss the brief flash of weakness.

"Stay safe," I tell them.

"You, too. I'll call when things settle down at home," Tobias says. "If we get a state of emergency notice, we'll have to close."

He briefly goes over how to lock things up, then leaves.

When I walk into the dungeon, I hear a sound that makes me freeze mid-step, as if someone waved a magic wand and halted me in place. It's a laugh. One that haunts my dreams and conjures up nightmares when it drags my past to the present.

It's just in my mind, I tell myself. There's no way she's here tonight. It's the memory that surfaced earlier that's playing with my head.

I cross my arms and stroll through the Dungeon. But I'm not really keeping an eye on safety like I'm supposed to. It isn't until the third brunette looks at me as if I'm crazy for staring at her that I realize, I'm looking for *her*.

She isn't here, though. I'd know that chestnut-colored hair. I'd know her deep brown eyes framed with thick black lashes and dark, beautiful skin. Hell, I'd know her scent from across the room.

I've got to get my head out of the past. I look at the bar. Fuck, I need a drink, but Dungeon Monitors don't drink while on duty.

A chorus of obnoxious phone alarms go off at once, including my phone, which beeps and shakes until I take it out of my pocket and shut it off.

Damn.

Blizzard warning in effect until six a.m. No on-street parking. Citizens are urged to avoid roads and get home as soon as possible.

That's my cue.

I text Tobias first then Brax and Zack, and in thirty minutes, despite some protests and reluctance from some members, we've completely emptied Verge. They head home, but I live a good distance away from here and don't want to risk the commute. Plus, I'm responsible for this place tonight, and even though it's vacant, I'm happier staying. My room is comfortable, and I have a change of clothes, food, and water.

It's actually kinda nice in here when it's empty. I double check all the doors and windows, then call Tobias.

"All clear?" he asks.

"All clear," I tell him.

"Thanks, man. Much appreciated, Axle."

We hang up, and I shut off all the lights. I'm heading to my room when I hear a sound that makes me freeze. I wait in the hallway, listening.

What the hell is that? And where's it coming from?

I follow the sound of the noise, then realize it's coming from the women's bathroom. *Shit.* I didn't even think to look in there to make sure it was vacated. And sure enough, as I approach, I hear a coughing sound and a whimper. I speed up my pace, shove open the bathroom door and freeze.

There's a woman kneeling over a toilet. The stall door is closed, and I can only see her knees on the cold tile. What the hell? Her skin is so dark in contrast to the vivid white tile, and the memory of earlier makes my pulse race. There's no way, though. It wouldn't even make sense.

"Hello?" I call.

I can see the bottom half of her body go rigid.

"Go away," she moans, then her body

convulses, and she retches. My stomach twists, but there's no fucking way I'm leaving. I step into the bathroom and wait until she calms. Something in me tells me to leave. If I keep pushing through, this isn't going to end well. My body vibrates with nerves, and I know that there will be no turning back after this. I push the door open. I know what I'm going to see before I do.

Chandra. Her head on her arm and eyes closed. Sick as a fucking dog.

"Chandra?"

Her eyes fly open.

"No," she whispers. "It's a nightmare. Tell me I passed out or I'm dead."

I huff out a mirthless laugh. "Nice to see you, too."

Chapter Three

Chandra

I want to die. I want the floor to open up and swallow me whole. Hell, maybe I *did* die, and this is some cruel punishment for not using my discretion and coming to a place like this. I died, and now I'm in hell.

After the second drink I had at the bar, my stomach twisted in knots, then morphed to a painful, dull ache. About thirty minutes ago, I found my way to the bathroom and thankfully just in time. I emptied the contents of my stomach, and even overcame my aversion for public bathrooms so I wouldn't puke on the floor.

Verge is clean, though, thankfully. Impeccably so. Still, kneeling on the floor with the cool tile at my knees is mortifying.

Maybe I caught a stomach bug. Maybe it was

something I ate. All I know is that I'm sick, violently and nearly instantly.

And then Noah walked in. Or at least someone who bears a striking resemblance to Noah.

But no. It's *got* to be him.

He called me by name, and I'd know that voice, those *eyes* anywhere. The man I fell in love with.

The man who ruined my life.

It's been seven years.

He looks so different now, though. He's covered in tattoos, and the hair I once knew as dark is speckled with gray at the temples. I thought he was a man when I knew him, but he's aged. Time has been good to him. His body is leaner, more defined and muscled, and he holds himself erect.

God, he was hot when I knew him. Now, he's grown into his looks and my belly tightens. He's beautiful.

I don't know if I can trust myself to speak.

"I don't go by Noah anymore," he says, and I recognize a firmness to his jaw I've never seen before. "Name's Axle. But we can talk later. What the hell are you doing sprawled out on the floor like this?"

I glare at him. "Examining your tile," I quip. "What do you *think* I'm doing, besides emptying the contents of my stomach and wishing for instant death?"

A corner of his lips quirks up, but he quickly sobers. "Let's get you out of here. Then, we talk."

I clutch the toilet. "If you move me, I could make you regret it," I say with a grimace. "I'm violently ill."

He shrugs and his voice drops. "Life is pain, highness. Anyone who says differently is selling something."

No. *Don't.* My mind pleads silently with him. He's quoting *The Princess Bride*. We watched that movie together until we could quote it back to front, and I'll never survive an onslaught of memories with Noah. It almost killed me when he left me, and he doesn't know what I did in the aftermath. How I saved him. How I killed myself in the process.

I can't help myself. I close my eyes and whisper, "What fresh hell is this?" It's my favorite quote from Jane Eyre.

But no. The old Noah and I related with literary lines. It's a closeness we shared that was dashed to pieces, and it's stupid and trite to conjure that up once more.

"I can't believe you're here," he says in wonder. Then his voice hardens. "Get the hell out of the bathroom."

I blink up at him in a daze.

He's glaring, his jaw hardened, and eyes narrowed on me. Oh, wow. I don't remember this side of Noah, but then I remember.

We're in a BDSM club.

Is he a… dom?

He shakes his head, stomps over to me, and hauls me up by the armpits to standing, then he lifts me into his arms. What the hell?

"Noah!" I protest.

"Axle," he corrects.

"I'm—sick. And I didn't give you permission to pick me up. Put me down!"

"No. I'm taking you to my room where there's a much more comfortable toilet should you need to empty your stomach again."

"Oh, ew," I say. "This is the most epically disastrous reunion known to man." I let my head fall back dramatically, which earns a chuckle from him.

"Damn, Chandra, you're just as cute as you were when I knew you."

Oh no he doesn't.

"Put me down," I whisper. "*Please.*" I can't stand being this close to him. The sound of his voice… his clean, powerful, masculine scent… the way he says my name, *Chandra*, like it's a prayer. It isn't a prayer, but a form of torture. We tried prayers, and they fell on deaf ears. I loved this man once, and I've had to put a wall up around my heart for survival. I won't let him tear that wall down. I can't.

"I'll put you down when I get to my room," he says. "You came into this club unescorted. Am I right?"

"Well…" I begin. "Not really. I came in here with Marla."

"Jesus Christ," he mutters. I blink in shock. The Noah I knew not only had no tattoos, he did not swear. What's happened to him? "And where's Marla now?" he asks.

"I told her to go home," I say.

His brow furrows. "And she just *went?* Just left you?"

"Well…" my voice trails off.

"Chandra," he chides.

"I… may have texted her and said I already went home," I whisper.

"So, you lied."

"Well, yes, but it was for her own good."

"It's still a lie," he says sternly, but before he can continue his lecture, my stomach lurches again.

"Noah," I moan.

He understands what I need and brings me to his bathroom. And to my utter misery, I christen it by emptying my stomach again. I want to die. I want to absolutely *die.*

He doesn't even grimace, though. He kneels beside me and holds my hair. When I'm spent and panting, he wipes my head with a cool cloth, then helps me to my feet and leads me to bed. It's so tender, my eyes water, but I tell myself it's just because he caught me at a weak moment. I can't fall for him. I loved once, and I can't go there again.

"Into bed with you," he says.

What?

"I need to go home," I whisper. My stomach churns, waves crashing on rocks.

"You'll go home eventually," he says with a sigh. "But tonight, you stay here. There's a blizzard warning in effect, and it isn't safe to travel, plus I want to be sure you're healthy again." He walks over to a refrigerator and removes a cold bottle of water. He opens the top, hands it to me, and orders, "Drink."

"I can't sleep here," I protest. The thought of being close to him, when I'm sick and weak, terrifies me. I need to be strong to resist his pull. Even now, when he's tender and kind and firm with me, I want to give in. I take a sip from the bottle just to appease him, and then lift my head and say with determination. "I must go home. Though I'm ever so grateful for your kindness, staying here is not an option."

His eyes narrow. "Why not? Why the hell would you *go*?"

Why *not*? Is he *high*?

"I don't owe you an explanation," I grit out, pushing myself to sitting and swinging my legs over the bed.

He takes a step close to me, and it dawns on me that we're in a BDSM club. Why is he here?

"Noah?" I ask, eying him warily. "What exactly is your role here, anyway?"

"No changing the subject," he says. "I said you're staying here, and I mean it. So first, we agree to that."

"No," I tell him, giving him the same heated glare he's giving me. "I said, I'm going home. We have a history, and I'm not—" I freeze and nearly bite my tongue to stop me from saying *I can't do that to myself again.*

I let him go. I had to. It was a necessary but brutal decision.

A little part of the old Chandra died when that happened.

He steps closer, his eyes smoldering. "You're not what?" he asks. He's so close, I feel the vibration of his breath on me. His voice, as rough as sandpaper, grates against my frayed nerves. "Letting me defile you again?"

"I didn't say that," I say, and to my horror, my throat tightens. "God, you can be an ass." Then my stomach flips and I barely make it to the toilet before I'm sick again. When I'm done, I wipe my mouth and close my eyes, not even bothering to stop the tears. This is miserable. It's painful. And I want to let the floor swallow me up whole so I never have to look into his beautiful, terrible eyes again.

"Chandra, come on now," he says softly. "I'll get you something in case you're sick again so you can rest in bed." He helps me to my feet, and I walk on trembling legs back to the bedroom. *I'm just weakened,* I tell myself. *It's just the situation.*

And I'm so damn sick, I can't stand it.

"What the hell happened to you, anyway? Is it just a stomach virus or something?"

I shrug. "No idea."

"Anyone you know sick?" he asks.

I shake my head. "Well, no." We reach the bed and I sink onto the mattress, grateful for the softness but mad that he's right. Like it or not, I can't go home. Not in this condition. I lay on my back and close my eyes.

"How much did you have to drink?" he asks, correction in his tone.

"Dude. Like two drinks? Not enough to make me this sick."

I can feel him glaring down at me even though I don't open my eyes.

"Who served you?" he asks.

"The bartender. *Duh,*" I say, waving my hand in the general direction of the door. "Travis?"

"Yeah." His voice is harsh, unyielding. "Anyone sit near you?"

I blow out a breath and roll to my side. "For God's sake. Who knows." I'm sick, exhausted, and here even though I have *no* interest in being here, so my patience is wearing thin. Not to mention the fact that I just met a ghost from the past who's making me feel happy and sad and wistful all at once. I can't look at Noah and forget the painful scars I've long since buried. So when I respond, my voice is angrier than I intend. Tight. Snarky.

"And who the fuck cares if someone was sitting next to me? What the actual fuck? Leave me alone, Noah."

His hand smacks my ass so hard and fast, it takes my breath away. My eyes fly open and I spin back around to look at him, which is a mistake since my belly clenches and aches.

"What the hell?"

He doesn't look even the smallest bit regretful or sorry. "The girl I knew didn't have a potty mouth."

"You should talk!" I protest, but my ass is burning from the sting, and to my utter horror, I'm way turned on, which shouldn't be possible in my miserable state. "You talk like a truck driver."

He just frowns and shakes his head.

"Well, you can't just *spank* me," I say, rubbing my ass. His gaze travels to where my hand rubs, and he swallows and lets out a breath.

"I smacked your ass. You're a little girl who's in way over your head."

"I'm not a little girl anymore," I protest through gritted teeth. "And I'm not yours to punish. That's how we got in trouble in the first place."

I don't mean to say it. I shouldn't have.

He leans down and even though his eyes still smolder, when he touches me, it's gentle and sweet.

"Get some sleep," he says. His voice hardens. "You're not leaving. If you try? I *will* take you straight over my lap and give you a real spanking. If you don't believe me? Do it."

There's nothing but sincerity in that gaze, and I know it to be true. I don't understand how this can both infuriate and excite me all at the same time, but it does. God, it does. My pulse races even as I clench my jaw.

He turns away from me and fiddles in the room, gathering blankets and clothes. I feel better now. My stomach has settled down, and I hope the worst of it has passed. Now that my stomach is slightly better, I'm so tired. It's warm and comfortable in here. I try to look around the room to see where he'll sleep, but my eyes are so heavy, I can barely keep them open.

He approaches me with a blanket and drapes

it over my body. "You need anything else?" he asks.

I shake my head. "I'm good," I whisper.

And as I float off to sleep, I swear I hear him say, "you always were."

Chapter Four

Axle

I watch as she sleeps. I can't help it. Her dark lashes flutter on her cheek as her eyes stay closed. Her skin's as dark and creamy as milk chocolate, her thick black hair shiny and full. Her parents— strict, demanding, and ruthlessly conservative— hailed from India. Though she was born and raised in America with not a trace of an Indian accent, she's a true exotic beauty, almost out of place wearing jeans and a t-shirt. She should be dressed in saris of emerald and ruby, magnificent swaths of luxurious fabric.

Her petite, curvy figure is covered under a blanket, and her shoulders rise and fall with slumber.

Why was she so sick? There could be many reasons, but I can't help being suspicious as her illness came on so suddenly and severely. Since

Club Verge lies at the heart of NYC, and though we vet our members and have strict protocols, it's not unheard of for strange things to happen here.

My own eyes are heavy with the need to sleep, but before I do, I want to be sure one last time everything's locked up tight. I go to the hall, which is vacant, and with a grim smile, check every bathroom and stall. No one's here. It's just me and Chandra. I shake my head and go to the dungeon. Everything's been put away. The tools and implements hang on the walls and in the cases as they're supposed to, already sanitized and replaced.

I lean against the doorframe of the dungeon and let my mind wander. What the hell is Chandra doing in a BDSM club? What has she tried?

What does she *want* to try? The image of her beautiful, curvy figure stretched over the cross or a bench assaults my mind. Part of me wants to wake her ass up and bend her over that spanking bench to punish her just for coming here.

I remind myself she's old enough. She can do this if she wants to. Then I grit my teeth and flex my palm, itching to punish her ass for darkening the doorway of a BDSM club.

When I knew her, she was a young little thing. Legal, but barely. Seven fucking years ago.

It was why her parents hated me so much. They wanted to press charges when they found out what was going on.

She was of age, though, and there was nothing they could do about that. Not legally, anyway.

They were fully capable of making her life a living hell, and fuck did they ever.

But I was a man of the cloth. Sworn to a vow of celibacy I broke so badly it was irreparable. I shake my head, trying to clear my mind of the thoughts that assault me from my past.

That was then. This is now.

I can control myself now. And controlling myself means not allowing the wicked thoughts that tempt to surface.

I give one more look around the room and shut the dungeon door and decide right then and there, the next time we open, I'm scening with a sub. Doesn't matter who she is, it just matters that she's unattached. Not looking for things like commitments and anything more than a one-night-scene. There are plenty single subs available and I'll seek them out. I need to exert my control over someone. I need to exorcise these demons and erase Chandra from my memory.

I groan inwardly. The best damn way to do that is to invite her to my bed. God. Why do I have to have such a goddamn hero complex? Shaking my head, I walk to the bar area and scope it out good and hard. The pool tables are bare and brushed, the floors swept and clean. And nearly everything at the bar looks good.

But when I walk closer, I see something a little amiss. I tip my head to the side and narrow my eyes, trying to hone in on the details. What is it? The counter's clear, the glasses neatly washed and put away. The bottles themselves look fine, and the stock of nuts we serve at the counter are covered and put away. What's amiss? It takes me a minute before I realize the video camera Tobias has trained over the bar is covered. It's so subtle, it's barely recognizable, but as a Type-A dominant, when I was hired for this position, I covered every single base. I went over the cameras with Tobias and made sure I knew how every one of them worked. Every member who steps foot into Verge signs an agreement that all but the private rooms are subject to video surveillance. Tobias keeps the feed on in his office.

I stand on one of the bar stools, frowning at the camera, climb onto the bar and tug at the black film that's covering the camera.

What the fuck is this?

I pull it off. It's a flimsy piece of opaque material. I hold it in my hand as if it holds the clues to what happened. Who did this?

I climb down off the bar and head to Tobias's office. The lights are off and the door's locked tight. I frown. He never locks his door when he's here, but he does when he leaves. Do I have the keys? I shake my head. This isn't my place to pry. I need to call the police. I could try Zoe or Zack, both officers with the NYPD and regular club members, but when I glance at my phone, I realize it's well past midnight. I tuck the fabric in my pocket and go to head back to my room. I nearly collide into Chandra, who's standing in the doorway.

"Jesus," I mutter, my heart slamming in my chest. "When did you come out here? And who the hell told you to get out of bed?"

She shrugs and her cheeks pink. "I wondered where you went," she said. "And what's the big deal about me leaving the room?"

"I told you to stay," I say with a frown, taking her by the elbow. "You need rest." The real reason is that I want her tucked away and kept apart from this place. I love Verge, but it's no place for a beautiful, innocent girl like her.

She lets me lead her back into the main bar area, but she's frowning. "And I listen to you why?" Her eyes are a little wide, though. She's trying to give me shit but she's a good girl and it doesn't come naturally to her.

"Because I have every tool at my disposal," I tell her. I'm barely resisting the urge to sit on a bench, swing her out and over my knee, and spank her full, beautiful ass right here and now. For talking back. For coming here. For being even more beautiful than I remember.

She frowns, but the pink in her cheeks deepens, as we make our way to my room. When we get to the dungeon doors, however, she freezes.

"Show me, Noah?"

"Axle," I correct. "Noah's dead."

She blinks and nods. "Okay. Axle," she says haltingly. "Since no one else is here, will you show me around the dungeon?"

Hell no.

"Not tonight," I tell her. "You need rest, and so do I."

Her full lips turn down in an adorable little pout. "Please?" she asks.

God, the power this girl has over me. She gives me puppy dog eyes and I almost cave.

"No," I say, more firmly this time. "And I've had enough of the back talk, little girl. Off to bed with you."

"I'm an adult, you know," she reminds me, but she allows me to lead her down the hall. She shrugs my hand off her elbow, though. "And we might be in a BDSM club, but I don't remember saying I'd submit to you."

"And I don't remember making that an option," I say. I rear my hand back and smack it against her ass. The second I do, I regret it. It wasn't even a conscious decision. My palm tingles and my dick hardens. God, I want to punish her so damn bad my mouth waters. It's breaking every BDSM club law in the book, not having her consent, but hell, there's something innate that calls me to her.

"Noah—Axle," she corrects in a whisper. She swallows hard. "You…" but her voice trails off. She wants to tell me off, but it's like she can't even talk.

I sigh. God, I remember how things used to be with her. It's probably my fault she's even into this shit. She was young and innocent, and I stole that from her. Showed her how delicious the loss of control can be with bondage. Awakened her inner submissive with punishment. Rewarded her with pleasure when she obeyed.

She liked it, though. And hell, I can tell just by the way she's looking at me, she likes it now.

"Bed," I say sternly, pointing at the door to my

room. My conscience tugs at me, though. "How are you feeling?"

"Fine," she says, then stifles a yawn. "Just tired."

I open the door to my room and tug her in, then walk her back to bed. "Good. Now get some rest." I release her, pull down the blankets, and pat the sheets.

"I should maybe undress?" she says, but she doesn't meet my eyes. I nod, then turn around to give her some privacy. The sound of a zipper. The rustle of fabric. I swallow hard and ignore the growing need inside me when I let myself imagine what she looks like undressing. I hear the bed creak and release a breath I didn't know I was holding.

Climbing back into bed, she lays her head on the pillow, and I tuck the blanket up around her. She fidgets a little but doesn't say anything. My mind is teeming with memories, and I can't stop them. I wonder if hers is, too. My heart squeezes. Some of those memories are painful. So damn painful. Even though it's against my better judgment, I lean over and stroke my hand through her thick, silky hair. Her eyelids flutter shut, and she sighs. I sit on the side of the bed, stroking her hair and rubbing her back until her breathing slows and her shoulders lift up and down in soft slumber.

This is wrong. So damn wrong. But I have to atone for my sins.

Chapter Five

———————

Chandra

I'm sitting on the steps, crying. I want to be alone. I'm nine-teen years old and live in a proverbial ivory tower, a gilded cage no one can enter. I wasn't allowed to go to college. I haven't been allowed to do anything. My mother and father have predetermined my future spouse already, and the knowledge kills me. I've never even kissed a boy, and yet I'm to be married.

I met him today, for the first time. He's serious. So very serious. But how am I supposed to spend the rest of my life married to a man who doesn't smile?

"He's a good provider," my mother says. "He gradu-ated top of his class and has already been offered a head position at his uncle's firm."

Great. A good provider. What exactly is it that she wants him to provide for me? Companionship and love are clearly not on that list.

My cousin married the man her parents picked out for

her, and she's… happy. I think. Sometimes it works out well. And sometimes it doesn't. How could it in my case? My parents don't know me at all.

"Hey," comes a gentle voice above me. I look up into the most beautiful blue eyes I've ever seen. Care and concern are written across his features, and to my demise, I read those before I see the stark white of his collar. Ice pulses through my veins. I shouldn't even talk to him. He's the new priest who moved into the rectory last week. We own the house two doors down from the rectory. My parents don't speak to the Catholics in this neighborhood, but they're aware that a new priest is in town.

No one told me he was young, and beautiful, and he has the eyes of an angel.

"Hey," I say, looking away. I'm ashamed of my tear-stained cheeks and swollen eyes.

He sits down next to me, a good distance away, but close enough like he's showing me his silent support. He doesn't know who I am or why I'm crying, but he sees someone sad and alone, and he chooses to stay. I turn away and get to my feet. I shouldn't be alone with any man, most especially not this one.

I go to leave, but his deep voice arrests me. "No," he says gently. "Don't run off. I won't hurt you."

I look at him in surprise. In my home, tears are a sign of weakness. It's unheard of that an emotional reaction like this garners sympathy instead of ridicule and chastisement. It's why I hid when I knew I was going to cry.

"Thank you?" I say tentatively. He gives me the ghost of a smile. It's so sad, but there's promise in it.

"You're welcome?" he answers my question with a question, and I laugh.

He reaches into his pocket and pulls out a tissue, then

hands it to me. I nod my thanks and take it. I blow my nose and tuck the tissue into my sleeve.

We sit in silence. I've always trusted my instincts, though. I don't know him at all, but deep down inside I know he's a man to be trusted. At the same time, I know this is wrong.

"It's my nineteenth birthday," I blurt out. I feel my cheeks warm. He didn't ask me, and I wonder if it's rude to offer this knowledge unsolicited.

"Happy birthday," he says.

I can't help but laugh. "Thank you."

Folding his hands atop his knees, he gives me a sidelong glance. "Something about that make you sad?" he asks. He's so much bigger than I am, and it looks almost funny that he's sitting on the stairs like that. He dwarfs them with his stature.

"My parents introduced me to my future husband today," I tell him. "I suppose it was a sort of birthday present."

"Oh?" he asks. His brows rise. "Is that right?"

He's trying not to judge, but this has clearly surprised him.

"Yes. My family still believes in arranged marriages. Few do anymore, but lucky me, my parents still do. It's safer, they say, and my parents have been planning my marriage for a number of years. Typically, it happens when a woman is eighteen and a man twenty-one, but they bent the rules, so I could graduate high school." I'm not sure why I'm telling this stranger my life story, but it feels right. And it feels nice to have someone to share my pain with.

"I see," he says, nodding. "I'm sorry, I wouldn't know anything about marriage," he quips, tugging on his collar.

I smile. It's the first time I've smiled in days.

"Me neither," I whisper.

We sit in silence for a moment longer.

"My name's Noah," he says after a time, extending his hand to me.

"Chandra," I say, and I take his hand.

His hand is strong and warm, the palm a little callused. When he touches me, my body does curious, wonderful things it's never done before. My heart races and my mouth goes dry. I don't even know Noah, but just touching his hand, I feel his innate strength and courage. To my surprise, his own eyes widen and the grip on my hand tightens.

"Chandra," he repeats, then swallows. "A beautiful name." He stops, and I know he's censoring himself. It isn't right for a priest to be talking to a young, sheltered girl like me. If anyone knew…

But he doesn't let my hand go. I wonder if he feels the vibe between us, the current of energy that moves from his hand to mine, as if something magical and wonderful transfers between us. And that's only from holding his hand.

"Yeah," I whisper. "Thank you."

He won't let my hand go, and I know if he does I might cry… again.

"Noah… can you imagine being married the rest of your life to a boring, dull, ugly person?"

He smiles his sad smile again. "No, Chandra. That sounds like Hell on Earth."

"Thank you," I say with a sigh. "It does."

I hear my name being called and the voice isn't far off. I yank my hand from his, suddenly vividly aware of what happens if we're caught.

"I need to go," I say, unable to hide the panic in my voice.

"Go," he says, gesturing for me to scurry by waving a hand at me. *"Be strong, Chandra. Until we meet again."*

I wake with a start and blink into the darkness of the room. The dream... no, the memory was so vivid, I can feel tears spring to my eyes. It takes me a minute to realize where I am and when I do, I keep my breathing quiet, and don't move on the bed. I don't want him to know I'm awake yet. Is he here?

I look around the room. When my eyes adjust to the darkness, I look down and see his body on the floor beside the bed. My God. He slept on the *floor* in the dead of winter? I peer over cautiously. He's lying on a blanket, with another blanket pulled up over his arms, dead asleep, like a watchdog keeping vigil by my bedside.

"Noah," I hiss. Then I roll my eyes. *"Axle."*

Who the heck gave him that name?

He shifts and grunts but falls back asleep. I reach down and shake his shoulder. "Hey. Wake up!"

He sits up with a start and blinks up at me.

I can't help but giggle. "Sorry," I whisper. "I didn't mean to scare you."

He frowns. "What's up?"

"For goodness sakes, it's freezing. Why are you on the floor?"

He scrubs a hand across his eyes and yawns. "You see any other beds in here?"

I sigh. "Well, you don't have to lie down there anymore."

He gets up and sits on the side of the bed. "What time is it, anyway?"

Pulling his phone from the bedside table, he clicks it on. "Jesus," he mutters. "Seven in the morning."

"Sorry," I mutter, not sorry at all.

He swipes his phone on and looks at the weather forecast. "Another foot of snow," he says with a whistle. "No one's going anywhere anytime soon."

My belly dips. I can't be alone with him much longer. He makes my pulse race. My mouth goes dry and hell if I haven't replayed that smack on the ass he gave me a dozen times. "Excuse me? Um, no. I'm going home today."

Frowning, he continues to read on his phone, then he puts it down and shoots me a stern but kind look. "Not sure about that. I'll call Tobias in a few." Looking down at me, his brows knit with concern. "You feeling any better?"

No, my mind says. But I know he's asking about my stomach.

"I think I'm fine," I say. "Must've been something I ate."

"Mm," he grunts. "Maybe. We'll see about that, though."

He's not buying it, but I'm not entirely sure I know why.

I watch as he heads to the bathroom, and when the door to the bathroom shuts, I'm alone with my memories. I close my eyes, and my mind fades back to a memory I've replayed over so many times, every single detail is vivid.

I walk into the darkened hallway, and Noah's pacing. Before he sees me, he runs a hand through his dark hair, making it stand up crazily, like a madman. I scared the hell out of him tonight. I was supposed to meet him at nine, but I got caught up with my friends and I'm so crazy late. It's two years after I met him, and I'm now twenty-one.

The man I was supposed to marry broke it off, to my immense relief and my parents' utter dismay. He eloped with a woman from Canada, and no one has seen him since. It would have been a blessing to me if my parents had seen it that way.

I snuck away, because my parents would lose their minds if they knew I was celebrating my friend's twenty-first birthday the American way. I told them I'd spend the night at a friend's house.

I didn't expect that I'd lose track of time, and when I finally decided to head to meet Noah, it was hours after we'd planned to meet. My parents don't expect me back tonight.

Noah's waiting for me. This is how we find time for each other.

When he sees me in the doorway, he freezes. His stormy blue eyes narrow and I feel the heat of his anger hit me right in the solar plexus.

"Where the hell were you?" he asks.

"I…" my voice trails off. This is very different from being in trouble with my parents. With him, knowing I'm in trouble makes my body pulse with electricity.

I've known him for two years. He's my confidant. My friend. It wasn't until I was twenty years old that he kissed me for the first time. Our relationship is wrong and it tortures him. I see it in his eyes, the way he fights to stay apart from me. I don't fight it, though. I'm not tortured. The day he kissed me, I knew I never wanted another man to touch me.

Noah is everything to me.

I swallow and walk to him with feet as heavy as lead.

He crosses the room to me, and we meet halfway. He tangles his hands in my thick, dark mane of hair, tugs my head back and bruises my mouth with his, a kiss so hard it takes my breath away. He pulls his mouth away and presses his forehead against mine. "I thought they took you from me," he says, a tortured whisper that makes tears spring to my eyes. "What the hell were you doing?"

I bite my lip.

"Chandra," he chides.

"I went out to celebrate Hailey's birthday," I falter.

"Why didn't you call me?"

"I don't know," I tell him. "They were drinking. I waited for them to call a cab or something, and I just lost track of the time."

He sets his jaw and takes me by the arm. I know what's coming. He's threatened me before and popped me on the ass, and hell if I don't want just this. I need to know what it feels like. I need to know he cares.

He sits heavily on the bench in the hallway, tugs my hand, and I topple straight over his lap, my legs dangling.

"Noah," I protest, my eyes closing tightly so I can handle the flood of warmth and fear that consumes me. "You can't." My protest is weak and futile, and I only offer it because I feel I have to.

He doesn't respond but pins my hands to my lower back and smacks his hand hard against my ass.

Apparently, he can. The stroke goes straight to my sex. I've been primed for this. He gives me four more firm strokes of his palm I feel straight through the thin fabric of my skirt.

"Noah," I groan. No one's here. No one will ever know what goes on between us. I feel like I need to protest, though.

With every smack of his palm, I squirm. I wonder if he knows this turns me on, and my cheeks flush at the mere thought. But when I wiggle on his lap, I feel his firm erection against my tummy and I know. It isn't just me who's turned on.

He stops, still holding me over his knee.

"When you tell me you'll come at a certain time, you will not leave me pacing here, worrying that someone hurt you when my calls go unanswered. That they took you. That you're hurting and alone."

Shit. My phone was on silent and I missed his calls. I tortured him with my irresponsible silence. Damn, I deserve a harder spanking than this.

"Yes," I whisper, and to my surprise, I automatically amend it to, "Yes, sir."

He gives my ass one final spank for good measure before he rights me. Taking my chin in his firm grip, his blazing blue eyes burn into mine. "Am I clear?"

"Yes, sir," I repeat, my voice shaky and taut with arousal. My panties are soaked, my heart stutters erratically, and I can barely remember my name. "I'm sorry, Noah," I whisper.

He brushes his lips against mine and when he whispers into my ear, I feel the vibration shudder through my body. "I'm sorry I had to punish you." But it's a lie. His cock's so hard against my ass I wonder if it's painful.

The door to the bathroom yanks open, tearing me from my memory. I'm turned on replaying it, but it isn't just the erotic vibe of that first spanking that affects me. It's more. The shared history brings me comfort, even if it's buried in pain.

That first spanking he gave me led to so much more. He tied me up and played my body with every twisted, kinky fantasy he harbored, as if having me at his mercy would exorcise his demons. It never did, though. The more he unleashed, the more he wanted. The more *I* wanted.

I was still twenty-one when he got me pregnant.

But he never knew that. By then, he was gone. And when I lost the baby, I could never bring myself to find him to share the tragedy.

"Let's get you something to eat," he says, crossing the room. He turns his back to me and goes to a little dorm-sized refrigerator that sits against one wall. Last night, I was overwhelmed and sick and I didn't really get a chance to look at the room like I do now. The bed is at the center, massive and comfortable. I look to the head and notice the posts with rings attached. My pulse quickens.

The bathroom is off to the left, and beside the bathroom door is the fridge, a small, circular table, and several cabinets. At the foot of the bed lies a chest, and beyond that, a comfortable sitting area with a small table with a glass top and a cabinet. I want to take a closer look.

"Chandra."

His stern voice arrests my attention. I blink up at him in surprise.

"I asked you a question," he says, blue eyes trained on me.

He's a member of a BDSM club and a dominant. My pulse races and I swallow hard, twisting my hair in my hands. I have so many questions for him.

"Yes?" I say, my voice little more than a breathy whisper.

He raises a stern brow. "How are you feeling?"

My heart aches, and there's a lump in my throat that won't go away, but that's not what he wants to know.

"I'm good," I say softly, looking away. "My stomach is fine now."

He's scowling but gives me an approving nod. "We're stuck here and can't get food anywhere else, but I've got some stuff that'll hold us over. I know Tobias has a few things on hand, too, so why don't we go foraging."

"Are you a dom at this club?" My words come out before I can stop them. He swings his gaze to mine, eyes narrowed, while he shakes his head.

"Babe, I'm talking about food, not role playing at a BDSM club."

Babe? My heart pitter patters. Role playing? It never was a role for Noah.

"Okay," I say stupidly, not knowing what else to say.

"Listen," he says. "After we eat something, you can ask whatever you want, okay?"

"Can you, um, turn away so I can get dressed?"

He nods and turns while I slip back into my dress. Then I slide my legs out of bed, bend down, and quickly make the bed. Then I run my hand through my hair and straighten out my clothes. When I turn to him, he's smirking.

"Need a broom? Want to give the floor a good sweep before we go?"

I stick my tongue out on instinct. His laughing eyes sober, and he shakes his head. "Still a brat."

"Still bossy," I quip.

He laughs but it's a little sad. "Honey, you have no idea," he says softly.

I turn away from him so he can't see the way he makes my cheeks flush. I use the bathroom and freshen up as best I can. I need a change of clothes, but he at least has a new toothbrush and travel-sized deodorant for me. I try not to think about why he has those things.

And then he's through the door and walking so quickly I need to practically run to catch up.

"Where are we going?" I ask

"Break room."

"I want to see the dungeon," I push, catching up to him. "Maybe I came to Club Verge for more than the excellent drinks and companionship. Has that occurred to you?"

I don't know why I'm being so difficult. He wasn't even arguing with me. He merely cuts his eyes to me. "Many things have occurred to me. And we'll address those things. First, we get food and I get in touch with Tobias. I check the forecast." He raises a brow. "And you'll behave yourself in the meantime."

I remember his palm smacking my ass the night before. I just nod.

I must be crazy. I never behave this way. What is it about him that makes the brat in me surface?

We cross through the bar area and head to a small room I didn't see before. It looked like a closet or something, but when he opens it, it's a break room of sorts. It's near Tobias' office. He ushers me in. There are two large vending machines here. One has beverages, the second snacks. There's a small circular table and four chairs, and counters behind the chairs.

"Looks like a regular office break room," I say with a smile.

"DM's often spend hours here," he says. "We sometimes get takeout, but there isn't always a lot of time. So, we have a break room and Tobias keeps it well stocked."

My stomach rumbles with hunger. I clutch it, and Noah—*Axle*—just smiles. He takes out a card and runs it through a slot on the machine then pushes a button and a drink slides to the bottom. He takes it out and hands it to me.

"Thanks," I say. It's orange juice. Cute.

"Something to eat?" he asks, gesturing to the vending machine, but I'm a little nervous now, and nothing looks really good.

I shake my head. "Actually, I'm good with just having the juice," I say. I fumble at the top but it's like soldered together or something because it doesn't budge. He reaches for it wordlessly, and I watch as his huge fingers grip the small can. He pops the top and hands it back to me.

"I wasn't suggesting, Chandra," he says. There's correction in his tone. A delicious shiver trills through me as my body remembers this. Him. All of it. The way he takes charge and cares for me in his calm, decided manner.

Noah. My heart aches for the man I once loved, and we're only standing in a damn break room with a vending machine.

It's more than that, though, and I know it. The present, right here and now, clouds the beautiful, heartbreaking memories, like frosted glass on a storefront window. All I need to do is lean in, breathe against the cloud, wipe it all away, and the memories will loom crystal clear and vivid. I can't deal with the way my mind and body are assaulting me with memories, and I try to get a handle on things.

He leans a hip against the counter and crosses his arms on his chest. Damn, the years have been good to him. When I knew him, he was younger and thinner, and though he had the same intensely blue eyes and stern jawline, the same wide breadth of shoulders and strength of stature, he was thinner, like a sapling reaching heavenward. The years have hardened his eyes a bit, and most definitely hardened his body. I tear my eyes away from him and look at the vending machine. It blurs, though. I see wrappers and cellophane. "Just pick something," I say with a shrug.

With a nod, he turns to me, swipes his card, then punches numbers. Little packets of food topple to the bottom of the machine. He reaches in to get them, then lays them down in front of me. There's a cereal bar in a green package with the picture of an apple, a cello-wrapped six-pack of peanut butter crackers, and a pair of toaster pastries wrapped in a royal blue package with silver edging. I reach for the toaster pastries and grin at him. My mama refused to buy these for me, but I loved them, so when I moved out on my own, I bought them by the caseload. He always gave me shit about it.

Now he just winks, and my stomach dips.

I tear open the package, pull out an iced pastry, and take a bite large enough I can't speak. I wash it down with orange juice, then take another bite.

"Not hungry, my ass," he mutters. He's gotten himself a can of coke which he swigs down before he tears open the cereal bar.

I wipe my mouth with the back of my hand and sip the juice again. "Glad there's a breakroom."

"Yeah," he grunts. "Except he somehow neglected the damn coffee."

I don't drink coffee myself, but I remember Noah always drank at least three cups of coffee a day.

"You always did like your coffee," I say contemplatively, polishing off one pastry and reaching for the second. My belly churns in satisfaction.

"I did," he says softly. "Still do. I guess some things never change."

Chapter Six

Axle

I shouldn't be looking at her mouth and imagining it wrapped around my cock. I like to pride myself on my self-control, but just looking at those full, luscious lips, the way she runs her tongue along the lower one when she's contemplative...

I shouldn't be staring at her full, gorgeous breasts, and wondering if she still has those dusky pink nipples that peak when I run my hands along her naked skin before I even touch them.

I feel myself sinking into temptation I've avoided for so damn long. This woman was always my kryptonite, but I'm no fucking Superman.

I joined the priesthood because I knew something was wrong with me. At least that's what I thought in my youth. It wasn't right to want to do twisted, sadistic things to another person. When I was in high school, I fantasized about taking girls across my lap and spanking them until they cried, cuffing their wrists, binding their ankles with rope. Fucking their mouths while their eyes were hidden behind blindfolds. It wasn't right that I'd slip my belt off before bed and imagine slapping the leather against a girl's full ass.

I didn't know back then that there were other people like me.

And when I confessed my depraved cravings in the darkest recesses of the confessional, I was told to avoid the temptation, not to dwell on impure thoughts. To fill my mind with prayer. After several years of trying this advice and failing miserably, I forced myself to join the priesthood. If something was wrong with me, I'd choose a life of celibacy. I would eradicate the perverted desires from my mind and cleanse my body with the sacraments.

I stayed chaste until Chandra and when presented with the temptation of her submission, her excitement when I dominated her... I couldn't say no. I fell headlong into my sadistic fantasies, and I found them even more addictive and tantalizing when I actually did them.

It was wrong, so wrong, and my conscience plagued me for defiling her.

Our break up was a mutual decision. She had a life to live. And I had to do the right thing.

I left the priesthood amidst shame and speculation, and I didn't look back. I left a black mark on my past, a smear of shame and failure. I chose damnation.

I pull myself back to the present.

She looks even more beautiful than I remember. Wide, dark brown eyes framed with impossibly black lashes, striking and feminine. Beautiful, creamy dark skin that fairly glows with a faint tinge of pink along her high cheekbones. Full lips that are naturally pouty, even at rest, a delicate little chin. Her figure is fuller than when I knew her, and I want to run my hands along the curves at her hips, the fullness of her breasts, her taut, beautiful ass.

She's nibbling her breakfast and sipping her juice, swinging her legs under the table like a little girl.

I reach for my phone and hit Tobias' number because I need to fill him in and hell, I need something to distract me.

He answers on the third ring. "Axle?"

"Hey, man."

"What's up?"

I fill him in on *almost* all of the details. I'll have to tell him about Chandra. He'll see the security footage when he comes in anyway. But now isn't the time.

"So it doesn't look like we'll be opening anytime soon," he tells me. "The city's ordered all non-essential business closed until further notice. Electricity's out in certain zones, and there have been four casualties alone in NYC. The blizzard warning is still in effect. Main roads are shut down. They're telling everyone but emergency personnel to stay off the roads."

"Jesus," I mutter.

"Do we still have power?"

"So far, yeah."

"Good. If we lose power, the heat goes down, too." He pauses. "So, man, one thing you need to know. I get all security feed routed to my home, too. For safety purposes. Nothing in the private rooms, as I've promised the long-term members. But the main areas are all under surveillance, and I keep an eye on things."

I know what he's seen, then. Hell, he could right at this very moment be watching me sit in this room with Chandra.

"So you know," I say. He knows I'm not alone.

"Yeah. Something you want to talk to me about?"

I glance over at her. "Yeah," I agree. "Can it wait until you're here?"

"Of course," he says.

I need to talk to him about more than Chandra, though. "I need you to go through that footage," I tell him. "But let's talk about that when you come in, too."

He sobers. "Sure, man. Everything okay?"

I remember the black covering on the surveillance camera above the bar. "I'm not sure," I tell him honestly. I want to know why that camera was covered and if it had anything to do with her being sick the night before.

I look at Chandra sipping her juice, and know I've got at least one long day ahead of me, maybe even several.

"Favor, though, man."

"Yeah?"

"Can you keep the footage in the dungeon and

bar area off while I'm here?" I don't want him laying eyes on her at all. Chandra belongs to me, and I want to secret her away. Just for my own eyes. Chandra cuts her gaze to mine and they go wide, but when she catches me looking at her, she looks away.

"Already done," he says.

"Much appreciated."

I'm not going to do anything with her, but I don't like the idea of us being under surveillance.

I hang up with Tobias and turn back to Chandra.

"What was that all about?" she asks. She wipes her mouth with a napkin and balls up her empty package.

"Checking in with Tobias," I tell her. "We needed to go over a few things."

"I see," she says thoughtfully. The she leans back and closes her eyes. "I haven't had something like that to eat in a good, long while."

"Good," I tell her. "That's total shit."

She opens one eye and peers at me. "The Noah I knew didn't swear." It isn't chiding, but more like she's confused.

I chuckle. "As if the Noah you knew was a moral man? No, Chandra. You misremember."

But her burning gaze tells me that's bullshit. She doesn't misremember a damn thing.

Tearing her eyes away from mine, she shrugs, but she's only feigning nonchalance. She feels this between us, the electric vibe of hunger and need that simmers beneath the surface, threatening to erupt.

"Well, anyway," she mumbles, and her voice is a little shaky and husky. She leans back and closes her eyes. "Those tasted delicious."

You tasted delicious, my body chimes.

God. Being in here with her is doing crazy shit to my head.

She opens both eyes and stares at me. "What happened to you?" she asks. "When did you leave the priesthood? I heard rumors, but I want to hear it straight from you." I don't expect her boldness, but I should. It's one of the things I loved best about her.

What happened to *me?* Besides losing every single relationship that meant everything to me?

She deserves the truth.

"I left the priesthood shortly after we broke up," I tell her. "I had no business being with you and you know it."

"Depends on who you ask," she says, looking away. "But we were consenting adults then." Her voice trails off. There's a pregnant pause, then her eyes come back to mine and she swallows. "We're consenting adults now."

I ignore the need to gather her up in my arms and kiss her into silent submission. I swallow, pretending that my whole world isn't crashing down around me, and continue. "I left the priesthood and went off on my own. Got into car repair." I should have chosen hard labor from the beginning instead of believing I could purge my sins with celibacy. I had no family to speak of and she knows that, but the priests I knew would no longer talk to me, parishioners naturally shunned me, and I needed to find my way. I deserved the shunning. I broke my vows. "I left our town and moved away."

"And I found you like a needle in a haystack." She smiles, but the smile is soft and sad, and her eyes grow wistful.

"Something like that," I say with a smile. "Now, your story."

Her eyes shutter, and she looks away.

"You can figure out mine, no?"

It's an evasion tactic, and now I need to know what she's hiding.

"No," I say, my voice taking on a stern edge that's natural to me. To us. "You tell me."

She looks back to me and lowers her lashes in submission. God, I missed this. She responds so beautifully to my commands. When I'd give her an instruction, she'd melt into me and cling, warming me through like sunshine. She thrived under my firm hand. Chandra was created to submit and flourished under my love and dominance.

"I don't want to tell you everything," she says, shaking her head. "Not now."

"Chandra," I warn. What is she hiding?

Her lower lip trembles. She always hated defying me, and she hates it now.

She takes in a deep breath and looks up at me. "I, too, did the right thing. I left my home. I broke off my engagement." She looks away. "I moved to NYC and went to school."

"When?"

"Four years ago."

Something's got a hold on my throat, it's tight

and I can't speak. The woman I love has been right here, near me, for years and I didn't even know.

I pull out a chair and sit down across from her. "What'd you study?"

"Writing."

Interesting. My girl always was a creative one, and my heart surges with pride that she claimed this for her own. "Yeah? What kind of writing?"

A corner of her lips quirks up. "I write romance," she says. "My parents don't know, of course. But I have three published novels, and I'm working on my fourth."

I blink. Her parents were modern-day Puritans and didn't believe in fiction, and she's written romance?

"It was… how Marla and I hit it off," she goes on, twisting her fingers together. "I don't know if you know this, but she has the largest, most comprehensive stock of kinky romance novels of any bookstore in NYC."

"Yeah," I say with a laugh. "Of probably any store in the world."

And then it dawns on me. Chandra writes romance novels and loves Marla's store for her kinky books.

I quirk a head to the side, both pleased and curious. "Do you write BDSM novels?"

Her cheeks flush a lovely shade, brightening her eyes. "Yes and no. Some aren't classic, consensual BDSM. Some are… Dubious consent. Darker."

Dubious consent? I don't even know what that

is, and I'm already hard. I adjust myself under the table.

"Under a pen name?"

She nods. "Of course."

"I want to read them."

"Noah—Axle… they're for women. And you'd be *shocked* if you read them." She crosses her arms over her chest as if to protect herself. "They're really dirty."

I laugh out loud. "Good girl," I approve. "Very good girl. If we weren't shut tight in here because of the snow, I'd be at Marla's today."

Now she's so red I bet she can feel her own cheeks flame but then her eyes grow concerned. "What do you mean, stuck tight in here?"

I tell her what Tobias told me.

"I have to go," she says.

I shake my head with finality. "You're not going anywhere. Not until it's safe." As if on cue, the wind howls like a mourning woman outside the break room window, and snow swirls heavily. She stands and peeks out the window. The streets are nearly vacant.

"Damn," she whispers. "But I'll bundle up and go anyway. I mean, I appreciate your protection and all, but I have things to do." She turns from the window and heads to the door.

"Yeah," I say, blocking her way. "And that isn't happening."

"Excuse me?" She tilts her head to the side. "Listen, just because we have history doesn't mean you get to tell me what to do. I won't drive or do anything stupid, but I *am* going home."

But my mind is made up. I wouldn't let someone I don't even know go out there. Chandra? No way.

"You're not going," I tell her.

The air crackles between us. I want to take her full mouth in mine and silence her backtalk. My palm yearns to smack her full backside and remind her of her manners, teach her some common sense. But I lost that privilege and I haven't earned it back. Not yet.

Then her eyes soften, and she smiles. It may be my imagination, but I see forgiveness in those coffee-colored depths. "If I'm not going anywhere, the least you can do is give me a tour of the dungeon?"

Chapter Seven

Chandra

It's like the air in here is laden with some sort of potion that makes me lose my self-control. Coming here was the first crazy thing I've done in who-knows-how-long. But I got sick of just writing the books. I told myself I needed a little research.

I have to get to work on my book, as I have a looming deadline and obviously didn't lug my laptop to the club. But the real reason I'm pushing to get out of here is because I need to get away from him. When I'm near him, I don't have any control over my body and my mind plays tricks on me. Every day, when I write my books, I'm fully submersed in the erotic pull of the power exchange. I've forgotten what it's like being around him. The way his voice makes my breasts swell and tingle, and the throb of need that pulses between my thighs. I want to feel the loss of control under his capable, trustworthy hands, the way we used to—

But no. I can't go back there. When he left, who I was shattered to pieces. When I was with him, my mind warred against what I wanted and what was right, but I couldn't deny how everything we did made me feel. I craved his protection and control.

When the pregnancy test came back positive, I couldn't bring myself to tell him. We were already done. I knew the swelling abdomen and tender breasts meant my body was housing the life of another, and that baby was his. I'd given him my virginity. I'd given him my heart. I gave him all that was me, and he lied to himself when he said leaving me was to protect me. Leaving me killed me.

I couldn't tell him about the baby because I was afraid he'd think it was a selfish, silly ploy to bring him back to me, and I was far too proud for that. So he never knew I was pregnant or that I lost the baby. He never knew the devastating pain that wracked my body and my heart when I said goodbye to my last connection to Noah. To a life that would never come to fruition.

Still bleeding, my heart lacerated, I took my meager belongings, and I left home. At first, I traveled like a vagabond, a college student living in youth hostels, funded by the money I'd put aside. My parents didn't pursue me. A daughter who left home was dead to them. And even though it hurt, I knew it was for the best. I thought he was back in my hometown, and since I never bothered to keep in touch with anyone from home, I didn't know he'd moved, too.

I left my past behind me. But I carried with me a deep, abiding craving for the lifestyle Noah introduced me to. I told myself that it was just how I was wired. It was part of my psyche. Raised by parents who were more enamored with the idea of me than the actual *me*, the logical side of my brain told me I craved his guidance because I lacked real care and concern in my youth.

I could never pursue the lifestyle apart from Noah, though. It lost its magic. And maybe I feel a little betrayed that he was able to. I did, however, fulfill every fantasy of mine within the pages of my books.

So when I asked him to take me to the dungeon, I pretended in my head it was for research.

"I'm on a deadline," I tell him. "And feeling very uninspired. Maybe you can show me around?"

He blinks slowly, his blue eyes trained on mine, stern and unyielding.

"For research purposes," he says.

I swallow. "Of course," I lie. "And anyway… didn't you ask Tobias to shut those cameras off?"

He quirks a brow and nods slowly to himself, mulling this over. My body starts heating, first in my chest, then the warmth radiates out to my arms and hands, then lower still to my legs and belly. I'm on fire, blazing hot with need and want.

When he speaks, it's soft and almost apologetic. "What kind of research do you need, babe?"

How far can I push this?

"Well," I begin. "I'd like to take a look at the equipment first." My voice sounds unnaturally high-pitched.

He nods and reaches for my hand. "Alright, then. Not sure what the hell else we're gonna do, stuck in here with a blizzard out there."

"Right," I agree, chattering like a songbird. "Exactly what I was thinking. I mean, unless you find a deck of cards or something..."

He squeezes my hand. "Deck of cards, my ass," he says.

"Hey, this is important." I'm serious now. "For real, this book is going to be my breakout novel. You'll see. Just wait and see what happens. I really did come here for research purposes."

"Yeah?" he says. We didn't plan it—well, I didn't, anyway—but we're falling into the easy camaraderie that was us when we were together, and I can't turn away. "You know… I think you *do* need a really thorough research day," he says. "For the sake of authenticity."

"Yeah?"

"Sure," he says. "Could be fun, you know. Plus, we're alone at a BDSM club. It's almost like it was fate."

"Fate," I whisper, my mind mired in our bitter past. But I shove those thoughts aside and allow myself to get a little excited about his proposition. "Okay. Huh. Well, what do you have in mind?"

"You be my submissive for today, and I'll show you what it's really like. Then you can take notes and bring what you learned to your book." He won't look at me, as if looking at me will shatter the moment.

"Submissive for the day," I say thoughtfully. God, I freaking love this idea. I don't have to commit to anything. It's all role play, with no real strings attached, and today is a day that almost doesn't count. It's eerily silent in here, insulated by the blizzard outside. No one is here to witness what happens. He's at work, and I will do my own form of work. Research. This isn't a commitment. It isn't even a date.

"What do you have in mind?" I ask.

We've passed the bar and now stand in the threshold of the dungeon. He releases my hand and turns to me. "Total submission," he says, blue eyes aflame with vehemence and excitement.

"Like your slave?" I sputter.

He shrugs. "Sort of like that, yeah." He flexes his fingers and nearly bounces on his feet, like a boxer in a ring, excitement rippling through him. "You'll submit to me. Do anything I say. You'll call me *sir* or *master*, and you'll wear my collar. I'll show you what it's like, but you'll have a safe-word." He raises a brow. "The consent thing may be dubious for your books, but not when you're with me."

We're role playing, I tell myself, willing my heart-beat to slow, to not fall for him again. This will be platonic and staged and there's nothing real about it.

"You'll never get a chance like this again," he says. Then his eyes darken. "And if you ever tried it with another man, I'd spank your ass."

My pulse races. "Oh?" I croak out. "I thought we were role playing."

"Full time submission is role play," he says. "I don't role play at being a dom."

I'm confused and excited and reluctantly hopeful.

"Alright, then," I tell him. "What's my safeword?"

He holds my eyes and a soft, sad smile plays at his lips. "Mad."

I know instantly why he chose it and the words fall from my lips unbidden. "The only people for me are the mad ones," I whisper.

"The ones who are mad to live," he continues. "Mad to talk, mad to be saved, desirous of everything at the same time, the ones who never yawn or say a commonplace thing…" It's one of our favorite quotes. Jack Kerouac.

"Mad," I repeat. "Got it." I look around the dungeon. It's shrouded in darkness, but sensual promises lie in the shadows. "And where do we begin?"

He smiles slowly, his gaze smoldering. Snapping his fingers, he points to the floor. "On your knees."

It takes a second for my body to catch up to my mind, and I drop to my knees. The ground looks like concrete but has a softer surface, and I don't feel the twang of pain I expected. I've never done this before. Never knelt before a man. And though something about it is so very wrong, like I'm subservient, I crave it and I have to shut off that part of my brain that wants to censor my actions.

This feels so damn good to have him standing over me while I'm in this submissive position. Something in me warms with satisfaction, like slipping into a warm bath.

"I'm going to teach you how to do this properly," he says, his voice gravelly but calm. In control. So very much in control. Reaching for my hair, he weaves his fingers through the thick, dark mass of it and coils it around his fingers. Instinctively, I close my eyes and sigh into the pull. *This.* This is what I want. "Back straight, little girl," he says, tapping firm fingers with his other hand along my spine, sending shudders through my body. I straighten my spine and look to him for further instruction. "Very good," he approves, fingers releasing the firm grip and massaging my scalp before he walks behind me. My pulse races as he inspects me in silence.

Standing behind me, I feel him bend down, his heat cascading over me like sunshine. "Bottom on your feet, just like this," he instructs, positioning my ass on the hells of my feet. "Good girl. And lay your hands in your lap. That's right. Now cast your eyes downward in submission."

Every instruction, given in his firm, strong voice, makes my pulse race faster. My panties are damp, and he hasn't even done anything sexual.

Or has he? Is this willful exchange of power innocent? I can't deny the erotic current that pulses between us.

I shouldn't do this. We have a past that we've

buried. We're not the same people we were back then. I'm no longer the virginal, sheltered girl and he's no longer the man struggling for purity and piety by purging his sins with denial. Now, we're willfully giving into this, our deepest, darkest cravings. Ones we began exploring so long ago.

But I don't answer to my past anymore. I don't answer to the expectations set on me in my youth, and I have nothing left to lose but my pride. And hell, if laying down my pride means fulfilling my primal desires, I won't stop now. If I do, I'll always regret opportunity lost.

And this is *Noah*. My Noah. The man who loved me, no longer bound by vows of celibacy and obedience.

Now the only call to obedience is my will bowing to his.

"Stay right there, Chandra. If I come back and find you've moved, I'll punish you."

The words *punish you* echo in my ears, travel down my spine, and throb between my legs, as I feel him walk away from me. Where's he going? What's he doing? I close my eyes, allowing myself to feel this moment so I can store it in my memory. My mind flutters with thoughts and questions about what he'll do to me, what he'll demand of me, but I will my mind to quiet. It serves no purpose to focus on what may happen. I need to live in the moment.

I've always been bad at that.

I stifle the desire to fidget by imagining my weight sinking into my heels. As I sit here in this submissive posture, my mind begins to quiet. I no longer hear the noise of the past or the whispers of the future but only his footsteps as he walks about the room gathering what he needs. I swallow the dryness in my throat and open my eyes when I hear him approaching me again.

Shrouded in light from the overhead fixture, I see nothing but his tall, muscular frame, all control and strength, strolling toward me with purpose in his eyes. In one hand he holds what looks like a single leather cuff. In another he holds a length of rope.

I shiver. I can't remember if I'm allowed to look at him or not so to be safe, I cast my gaze downward.

"Eyes on me," he directs, answering my question. I look at his eyes and imagine they're filled with warmth, but I dismiss that thought. We're role-playing. This isn't real. And this is research. I'll take what I learn here and weave it in my books for authenticity.

"Before we begin," he says, coming to a stop in front of me, "we talk hard limits."

I swallow.

Crap, he knows what he's doing. This is like a scene taken right out of one of my novels, and I can't help but shiver in delight and anticipation.

"Okay," I say tentatively.

"I say what I want to do, and you say green or red. Red means a hard no."

I nod. I can do this. It's easy enough.

His eyes grow molten. "Spanking."

I swallow. "Green."

His lips twitch.

"Whipping."

My heart rate spikes. I clear my throat. "Green."

He laces his fingers behind his back and stands, tall and powerful, over me.

"Nipple clamps."

"Green."

"Anal plugs."

My voice is choked. "Green."

"Medical play," he says and I give him a curious look so he tips his head to a table that looks like it belongs in my OB's office.

Shit. Ok well I trust him, so… "Green."

He nods slowly. "Violet wand? Electric stimulation," he explains.

Oh. Wow. Okay. "Green."

"Wax play."

Fuck yes. "Green. So much green."

He releases a low, dark chuckle. "Rope play? Bondage?"

I lick my lips. "Green." My panties are soaked. My thighs rub together, and I want to feel his pressure there. Something. Anything.

"Knife play."

I swallow and shiver and think before I reply. "Green."

Leaning down, he draws his thumb down the side of my cheek and cups my chin in his warm hand. "You're doing very well, Chandra. You're holding position and answering me promptly. Good girl. You'll be rewarded for that." My heart sings. He holds my chin between his thumb and forefinger, my gaze locked on his. "But from now on, you remember to say *sir* after any response."

I nod. "Yes, sir."

Oh, God, it feels good to call him sir, and I don't understand why. But my vision blurs with unshed tears and I want to feel his gentle hand once more.

He walks away from me and retrieves a long, thin black implement from a nearby shelf. There's a small square of leather at the end. A riding crop. Tamer on the spectrum of BDSM toys, but capable of packing a good, solid sting.

He flicks it against his hands as if testing it, then walks behind me. He doesn't move at first. "Keep position, Chandra," he says. "Rate it," he instructs. "Scale of one to ten, tell me how much this hurts." I nod, then immediately feel the sharp sting of the crop to the upper part of my ass, just where my heels hit my bottom. I flinch, but the sting quickly fades to warmth, sending a tingling sensation between my thighs.

"Three?" I ask.

He gives me a harder whack with the crop. "Seven!" I pant.

"Only seven?" he says, which surprises me, right before the third smack falls, the most painful one of all, a flare of pain that takes my breath away.

"Eight," I croak out. It isn't a ten. I know there are things here that will be far beyond that ten.

"Chandra," he chides, warning in his voice. "What did I tell you comes after every response?"

"Sir," I say. My body is molten, my ass stinging, and my feet are beginning to fall asleep.

"Good," he says.

"Sir?"

"Yes, baby," he says, running a hand along the back of my head.

"My feet are beginning to fall asleep."

"Up you go, then. We'll continue this over the spanking bench."

Oh my God. I've been dying to try one of those ever since I saw them the night before.

Taking my hand, he lifts me to my feet and walks me over to a spanking bench in the shadows. It's padded where my belly lies, and there are cuffs at my wrists and ankles.

"I'd prefer to have you in a submissive position when we go through our limits," he says. "It'll get you more readily into the proper headspace."

"No argument from me," I say. I mean, I'm practically leaping out of my skin with excitement. It shocks me when the crop whistles through the air then lands on the fullest part of my ass in a punishing swat.

"Correct response."

"Yes, sir," I amend. "This will take a while for me to remember."

"It won't," he says. "Because if you forget again, I'm giving you a proper spanking."

Ahhhh, my head says, incapable of thinking much beyond that because he's already positioning me over this bench.

"Sir?" I ask. "May I ask you questions?"

"For now, you may," he says.

"Well, who invented this thing? I mean a lot of things have more than one purpose, right? Cuffs are for prisoners. Crops are for horses, too, and things like… stocks, or a whipping post, or even an exam table has another purpose. But a spanking bench? I mean, it's like a fork. There's only one purpose."

He's fastening the leather cuffs around my wrists, first the left, then the right, then my ankles are bound below me. I push and pull against the restraints because I need to feel them. I'm not sure why, but I like not being able to move freely with him standing over me.

"That I don't know," he says. "But I know it's one of the oldest tools we have and was likely borne of a good need.

"It's a little crazy," I whisper.

"You're a little crazy," he counters.

"Yeah," I whisper.

I shiver when I feel his touch start at my shoulders then work all the way down my back, to my backside, then to the tops of my thighs. He's holding the crop over me to make sure I respond correctly.

"Breath play," he asks.

I know what that is, and it scares me, but I'm not going to back down. "Green, sir," I tell him.

He leans down and whispers in my ear. "Chandra, you don't have to try everything. It's okay if you want to say red."

"I don't want to chicken out," I tell him. "Plus, you gave me a safeword. If I chicken out, I can safeword, right?"

"Yes," he says, straightening. "Alright then. And if you're gagged, I'll find a way to make sure you can still safeword."

"Thank you, sir."

"Water play," he says, and for the first time, horror strikes me, and it takes me right out of the moment.

"Red, sir," I tell him.

"Good girl. Gags?"

"Green, sir."

"Public punishment?"

"Oh. Green, sir."

"Public sex."

Holy hell. "Um. Yellow, sir?"

I cringe, wondering if I'll get in trouble for not following the rules, but he only chuckles.

He goes through a few more, and I'm not sure what everything is, so I ask, and find there isn't much I'm not at least willing to try. I do wonder, though. How much is *he* willing to do? Are any of these things off *his* limits? I don't know.

"You've done a very good job," he says. Then he's gone. I try to look around, but he's slipping something silky and black over my eyes. "God, you're a vision," he says, his voice choked with… what? Emotion? Desire? I don't know.

"Thank you, sir," I say, and then I'm sinking so deep into the darkness it's beautiful and scary and exhilarating. I let my weight sink into the table, and for some reason, the bonds at my wrists and ankles no longer feel restrictive but liberating. I've allowed this. I've let him put me in this position, and here, engulfed by darkness, movement disallowed, I can only feel.

"Clear your mind, Chandra." His words are beside my ear, and the warmth of his breath makes little goosebumps prickle along my skin.

"How do I do that, sir?" I ask. "My mind is constantly going."

Smoothing a hand over my hair, his voice is at my ear again. "That's a very good question, baby. Start by just feeling."

Fingers tangled in my hair at the base of my scalp. He weaves and tugs, sending a shiver of delight along my skin, then strong, firm fingers are massaging my skin. It's soothing, like getting my hair washed at the salon, and almost as nice as warm water trickling over my hair.

"Imagine your thoughts quieting," he says. "Every time I touch you, they seep out of you like the tide ebbing at sand." His hands are at my neck, kneading so firmly it's almost painful, then one hand wraps around my throat. "Just *feel*," he instructs. His grasp tightens and my breath hitches. I can breathe, but barely, and I need to focus hard against rising panic. My pulse races, my body tensing, then he lets my throat go and both hands are at my shoulders. He runs them along my body, down my sides, and when he gets to my ass, he yanks up my dress.

"Noah! *Axle.* Sir!" I protest.

"If you're obeying me today, you'll lose your clothing when I command it," he says in a deep, chiding tone.

I whimper a little but nod. "Yes, sir."

"You're new to this, and that's okay. But sometimes if you're new, you push yourself further than you should. I need to keep tabs of my marks on you. You'll lose the panties so I can see."

I'm swimming, sinking, drowning. His fingers gliding up to grasp the strip of fabric. My hitched breath. The touch of his warm, rough hands yanking my panties down and over my feet.

God!

"Yes, sir," I say. I'm lightheaded and it's hard to breathe, but my core contracts with his command.

"Chandra?"

"Yes, sir?"

"Breathe," he instructs, then something whistles through the air and lands on my ass with an audible *snap.* I yelp, and try to get away from the burning sensation, but I can't move. This is definitely not the crop, but something far more painful.

"There are a few things that can really help aid your submission," he says. One warm hand presses firmly against the small of my back, before another burst of pain flares against the underside of my ass. "Things that will heighten my dominance over you. One is a good, hard spanking." He spanks me again, and again, and I can't think beyond the pain.

"Remember your safeword," he warns me before he spanks me again. "What is it?"

"Mad," I whisper, the irony hitting me with its force. I'm mad. He's mad. Everyone who sets foot in this place is mad, wanting to play with pain and power and getting off on what should be something to be avoided. My mind shuts my thoughts off when he spanks me again, this time harder, but the pain quickly fades to warmth.

"Mad," he repeats. Then he's spanking me in earnest. For some reason it doesn't hurt as much now, though. It's still painful but my body absorbs the pain, and I arch as much as I can tied to these restraints. I need more. I want deeper. Harder.

He pulls away from me only enough to elicit an involuntary whimper, then he's back with something else harder, and though the burn fades quickly, the pain is deeper and somehow even more humbling. The loud *whack* echoes in the small space, and my clit throbs with the impact.

"Good girl," he approves. "You're doing such a great job. Let go. Release it. *Feel*, baby."

And I do. I feel the touch of a man who once loved me. Who maybe loves me still. And I can't remember what happened or where we are or even why. My thoughts are jumbled and confused, but there are tears in my eyes. It isn't from the pain, though, but something deeper that he's drawn to the surface with this pain, and I hate it. This was not a good idea.

His voice sounds so far away. "That's it," he says. He's kneading my bruised, punished flesh with his strong hands. "Such a good girl," he approves. Tears fall freely now, and he brushes them away with one hand. I'm still submerged in darkness behind the blindfold, but it only makes me more aware of everything around me. His heavy breathing. How strong and powerful his hands are as he kneads my bare skin. The way my core tightens and contracts when his hands brush the inside of my thighs.

His hands are at my ankles and the cuffs are undone. My ankles are free, my wrists still bound, and then I'm in his arms and his mouth is at my ear, his voice soothing and a little sad. "Time to role play a little aftercare."

Chapter Eight

Axle

Watching Chandra stretched out on the bench, I want to lift her in my arms and tuck her into me, so deeply and securely she can't ever flee again. She's still blindfolded, but the blindfold is damp with her tears and they're seeping beneath the edge. I brush them away and unfasten the cuffs at her wrists so I can draw her to me.

When I offered to show her what this was like under the thin guise of research, a warning twang in my gut told me this was a bad idea. I knew I'd get turned on dominating her. I knew I'd deal with a raging hard-on and the inability to eviscerate the memory of her from my mind tonight, tomorrow, maybe ever. But I didn't think of how this would affect *her*.

She always was an emotional girl, a sweet little thing who wore her heart on her sleeve. She's strong, though. So damn strong. I've seen her withstand pain that would've made others crumple, then rise above when others failed.

But when she cries, she undoes me.

When she's completely unrestrained, she lays on the bench like the good girl she is, waiting for me.

"C'mere," I say, my voice gruff in the quiet room, belying the tenderness that warms me through. She fumbles at the blindfold.

"No," I instruct. "Leave that for me."

Her hands obediently fall to her sides. I pull her head against my chest and unfasten the blindfold. The damp, silky fabric falls to the ground. I kick it to the side and pull her to me. She folds into my chest easily, as if she was meant to be there, and here, in this moment, I know the truth in a way I never did before: she *was*. She was meant for me, and I fucked that up.

Our decision to break up was mutual, but hell if it wasn't a mistake.

I left her once. I won't do it again. When the snow clears, and she leaves, I could let her vanish into the vastness of NYC.

I can't let that happen.

I don't know what it will take to bring her back to me but holding her vulnerable form against mine is a goddamn start. She fits so easily against my chest, soft and sweet and tender. I kiss her forehead and brush the hair back from her face, then take her hand and lead her to a nearby bench. I sit down and pull her onto my lap.

I half expect her to protest, but aftercare is

often part of a scene, and if she doesn't like this, she has her safeword. But she says nothing. Not a word. Even her tears have stopped, and now she just lies her head on my chest, one hand splayed gently against my shoulder, the other tucked up against her. We sit there in the quiet, while I run a hand along the back of her head.

"It's intense, huh?" I ask her.

She nods. After a moment, she says, "Wouldn't be as intense if it were with someone else, but yeah. Intense is a good word."

Something in me warms at that, but at the same time my mind tells me *stop. Run. Danger zone.*

"Those little spankings I gave you when we were dating were nothing like that," I say. "But boy did I want to give it to you a time or two."

Her laughter tickles my ears, and my arms involuntarily tighten around her. "I know. And I maybe deserved it a few times."

"That time you went out with your friends and got in trouble down by the beach?"

She's giggling against me now, her eyes still bright with tears but now crinkled up with laughter. "You brought me home and threatened to redden my ass if I ever did that again. Oh you were so mad. I felt terrible. But you know, I fantasized about that threat for years."

"Did you?" Why does this surprise me? She always melted into me when I swatted her ass, even if sometimes she feigned indignation.

"You actually *did* punish me once," she tells me.

"Did I?" I can't remember.

"How can you forget something that's seared into my memory like that?" she asks, half amused, half angry. "Yeah," she says. "You know, I write about this now. I get why I was drawn to it. Heck, I get why I'm drawn to it now."

I hold her in my arms. I could do this forever. Just hold her while she talks to me.

"Yeah? Tell me."

She opens her mouth, then shuts it again. "Are we still scening?"

The question surprises me, and I feel my brows rise. It isn't time to reminisce. Not now.

"Yes," I tell her, letting her go. "Feeling better now?"

She nods, and her eyes shutter a little. "Yes, sir. And I will tell you, just maybe in a little while."

I question whether or not I should make her obey me. There's one stray tear on her cheek I wipe with my thumb. And when she looks at me with those beautiful doe eyes of hers, her full lips parted and cheeks bright pink, I can't help myself. I lean down and brush my lips against hers. She moans into my mouth, and my cock thickens at the sound. Jesus, God I missed this. Chandra's breathy moans. Her responsive body that craves my touch, my dominance. Her soft, sweet body yielding to mine. My body remembers this, how right and good and natural this is.

I'm suddenly aware of her skirt that's tucked up at her waist, and the heat of her skin against mine and the way her full breasts heave against my chest. I groan into her mouth when her tongue laces against mine. I grip her scorching hot ass in one hand and brace her with the other, but I need more. My lips punish hers with the heat of a thousand past hurts, branding her for being the temptation that broke me, that breaks me now. I reach for her dress and yank it up further, palming a full breast before I tweak her nipple to punish her more. But this is a sweet, seductive punishment.

I can't do this with her again. I took advantage of her once. I refuse to allow myself to do it again.

It takes every bit of self-control I have to yank my mouth away.

"Why did you leave?" she whispers.

"You told me to go," I respond, my voice tortured and strangled. Fuck, I don't want to talk about this now. Not ever.

"You shouldn't have listened," she says, but I'm still the damn dom here, and I'm not letting this go.

"Enough." I silence her with a harsh command. Her lips close tightly, and her eyes flash at me, but she doesn't disobey.

I let this aftercare get out of control.

We aren't the people we were back then. We never will be again.

I promised her a day of role play. Fuck if I'm gonna let my weakness keep me from doing exactly what I said I would.

"We're moving on," I tell her. I weave my fingers through her thick, black, fragrant hair and pull her head back. When my cock twitches at the way her mouth parts and her pupils dilate, I welcome the punishment. I ache to fill her, to plunge into her to the hilt and take what's mine.

But I won't. I lost that privilege. I'll torture myself by meeting her needs and neglecting my own, but I'll remember. Let it cleanse me.

Holding her hair in hand, I lean in and grate against her ear. "Back on your knees."

She falls to her knees, both apprehension and excitement written in her features.

"Good girl," I approve. "Kneel the way I instructed you."

She's clumsy, nearly tipping over, and she frowns at me. I lean down and help her by placing her in position. When she kneels like a good little sub, I smile at her.

"That's it, baby. Just like that." I stand and walk to where I have a stash of new equipment at my disposal. I palm a delicate pair of lavender clamps and a jeweled plug.

If she wants to see what this is like, I'll show her.

She's keeping position, but her eyes follow my every move, and when she sees the metal toys in my hands, her eyes go impossibly wide and her lips part.

"Axle," she whispers.

"Sir."

"Sir, I…" her voice trails off and I give her a hard look. If she doesn't want me to do something, she safewords. If she doesn't, I'll have to teach her.

I sit on the bench in front of her and eye her pointed nipples against her dress. The dress has to go. I reach for the hem and lift it up. "Up you go." I guide her arms up and strip her. Folding it, I place it on the bench next to me.

"Good," I approve. "Now the bra."

She unclasps her hands and reaches for the bra, her hands trembling, but it's hard on her knees to get it right.

"Hands back in position," I instruct, then I reach down and unfasten the bra at her back. Her full, voluptuous breasts swing free. I stifle a groan at the sight of those dusky pink nipples, impossibly more beautiful and tempting than ever, the hardened nipples that beckon me to lick and suckle and nip them. Cupping one breast in hand, I lean down and run my tongue along the peak of the other. Her head drops back, and she moans, melting into my mouth. I reward her with my fingers at her pussy, and when I feel her wet folds, I stroke her as a reward for being such a good girl. She's primed now. Perfect.

Too soon, I tear my hands away and take out the nipple clamps. I keep my eyes on hers when I fasten the clamps. The coated lavender metal hangs in a loop connecting the two clamps. With a gently swipe, I pull the chain, causing the clamps to tweak her nipples. Chandra whimpers and her shoulders rise, mouth parted.

"Just like that," I tell her. "Keep position."

Running a finger along the metal edge of the chain that binds the clamps, I let the gentle sway of metal tug them. I fastened them firmly enough to stay but gentle enough that they won't harm the tender skin. When I tug a little harder, she hisses and rises, but when I bend down and smack my palm against her ass, she falls back in position. I hold the jeweled plug up for her to see.

She swears under her breath, which earns her a good, hard swat to the ass. She quiets.

What happens when she leaves here today? Will she come back like she did last night, and give her submission to someone who isn't worthy of it? Hell, *I'm* not worthy of it, and here she kneels, naked, and vulnerable, and the safeword hasn't left her lips.

I hate the idea of her submitting to someone else. If another man lays eyes upon her when she's vulnerable and split open, I can't hold myself accountable for what I'll do.

I want her to safeword. I want her to know she doesn't have to take what I give her, and that when it's too much she has the power to stop me. There's almost nothing on her hard limits, but hell, there should be. No one should take advantage of her. She controls the power here with her consent, and hell if I'm going to let her fall into this without knowing exactly what she's getting into.

"Exam table, Chandra."

She blinks.

"Exam table?" she repeats.

I feel my lips thin in disapproval. I don't want her repeating the instructions, I want her moving. I can feel anticipation weaving its way through me and I'm so damn hard it aches, but I have to keep myself calm and in control.

It isn't her fault she's desperate for domination.

It's mine for showing her this to begin with.

But hell, the girl needs to know what could happen to her.

Stumbling clumsily to her feet, she quickly rights herself and winces when the clamp chain swings, tugging her delicate nipples. I palm the weight of the chain in my hand to momentarily alleviate the pressure.

"I'm not going to warn you again to safe-word," I tell her. But hell, I just did.

She nods, and there's something in her eyes that puts me back years. She's older now, but her eyes haven't aged, and when she looks at me like that, I'm still her secret lover, and she's still the irresistible beauty I'd have given anything for.

That's bullshit. You wouldn't give anything for her. You left her.

But it was for her own good.

Her own good, or yours?

I silence the mental berating with force, focusing on what I need to do next.

Her steps are lazy and slow, as she eyes the paper-covered table with apprehension.

"Sir?" She bites her lip and gives me a sidelong glance.

"Yes?" God, I love when she calls me that.

"What happens on that table?" she asks.

"No exam tables in your books, Chandra?" I know I'm borderline mocking, but I want her afraid.

She shakes her head, thick dark hair tumbling about her bare shoulders. But the movement makes the clamps swing and she winces a little.

"Anything I want, babe. Up on the table, lie on your back and spread those knees."

This isn't even my kink, but I've seen enough

scenes to know how this can go down. I also know it's something that's just beyond her comfort zone enough it very well may pull that safeword I want out of her.

She climbs gingerly on the table, trying not to make the chain swing, but when she's on her hands and knees, I snap my fingers. She freezes.

"Sir?"

"Keep position, Chandra," I instruct, giving her ass a good crack as a good reminder. I reach for an unopened bottle of lube, and coat the plug. I never thought this was something that would appeal to me and chose it specifically to push her beyond her comfort zone, but when she presents her ass to me, my dick swells. I lick my dry lips and swallow as I approach her.

"Chest down, baby," I instruct with a hand on the small of her back. She obeys, hissing when the clamps come in contact with the paper-covered surface of the table. When I circle her tight bud with the lubed tip of the plug, her chest flies off the table, but I remind her to obey with a stinging smack to her ass. She falls back to the table and whimpers.

"Relax," I instruct. "I chose the smallest one we have, and you can handle this."

I insert the very tip, gently at first, then with more power. I've done this enough times I know how to ease it in. She should be good and uncomfortable now. When the plug is fully inserted, I take a moment to admire the way the beautiful jeweled top looks against her dark, soft skin. I've stripped her, spanked her, clamped and plugged her. She's either way out of her comfort zone, nervous with anticipation, or ready to fly. Maybe all of the above.

"Now on your back," I tell her. "Be careful."

Gingerly, her ass tight with the plug and her nipples taut with the clamps, she gets on her back obediently.

I want her to safeword, but I can't help wanting to reward her for this.

"Such a good girl," I tell her. Reaching down, I brush the now-damp hair off her forehead and kiss her temple. "I'm taking the clamps off during this scene. Stay still while I do."

Removing the clamps is when the real fun begins.

She trembles, and it pulls at my heart a little, but she needs this from me. When I remove the first clamp, her mouth parts and her eyes go half-lidded with the rush of blood that returns to her abused nipple. I bring my mouth to the punished peak and gently take it between my lips, suckling and licking as the blood flows back.

"Ahhh," she says in a strangled cry. I take her mind off her nipples by gliding a hand between her thighs and stroking her soaked folds.

Releasing one nipple, I remove the second clamp. This time she whimpers but holds position. I give that nipple the same treatment, until her breasts are pink and full, and her lower body trembles with want.

"Taking good mental notes, I hope," I quip.

"So damn good," she groans. Then her eyes

flash. "I can take better notes if you make me come." I slap her thigh, hard.

"When I'm good and ready," I tell her. "You need to remember your place, Chandra. I have some questions for you. Do you ever dabble online? Online kink forums or groups?" I know Marla does, and I wonder if Chandra does, too.

She frowns at me. Good. Now we're finally getting somewhere. "That isn't your business," she says.

Instinctively, I pinch her inner thigh, and she lets out a little scream. "Axle!"

I pinch her again. "That's sir."

"Sir!"

"Yes?"

No damn safeword.

She just glares at me.

"Don't give me that look. I asked you a question. Now unless you want a spanking across that pussy of yours, you'll answer me."

Blinking furiously, her eyes dark and stormy, full lips pulled down in a glare, she grates out, "Why do I need to answer you?'

I'm a man of my word. She'll learn that.

I lift my hand and bring it down on her shaved pussy firmly, not enough to injure, but hard enough she'll remember this. She flinches, but she still doesn't fucking safeword, just whimpers a little, and now a sheen of arousal gleams on her inner thighs. I'm pushing her hard, and she fucking loves it.

"Do you or do you not give your real name online?" I ask.

She clenches her jaw and her eyes shine bright with tears, while at the same time her legs tremble. "Yes," she finally says.

I spread her legs and take my place between them. "Don't ever do that again," I tell her. "You ever give your real name to an online dom and I'll take my belt to your ass. There are too many people who'd revel in hurting someone like you." Beautiful. Trusting. Naive. "Understood?"

She's panting and quaking, but she nods her head vigorously. "Yes," she says. "Yes, sir."

"Good girl," I tell her. Leaning in, I kiss the tender, damp skin between her thighs. "Now for your exam."

Chapter Nine

Chandra

I knew he had it in him. I knew there was a devious, twisted, salacious mind behind those kind eyes and witty tongue. He kept himself back from me, letting out his inner demons so rarely that I only caught glimpses. I knew he craved feeding me pain and controlling me, and that he held himself back.

Now, here, while I'm strapped to this table and at his mercy, I can see how he's embraced the sadist within, and hell I want this.

I want to hurt, and I'm not sure why. I can't fathom the idea of random pain, but carefully meted out at the hands of the man I trust is something altogether different.

My body tingles and pulses beneath him, every nerve a live wire of anticipation, sizzling and snapping with energy. When he drags his silky mouth and rough whiskers along my inner thighs, I moan. He licks and suckles my skin, and my pussy tenses with need. My tortured nipples throb, full and peaked from the punishment and pleasure he's inflicted.

Reaching for my ass, he squeezes the punished skin, then he shifts his hand to where he's plugged me. I feel so damn full. I need to climax.

"Sir," I whimper. "Axle."

"Your breasts are perfect," he says, leaning in just to touch his tongue to one peaked bud one at a time. Then he pulls away and continues his inspection. "A beautiful pink pussy that needs to be punished," he says thoughtfully, while he runs his hand between my legs.

"Punished?" I ask, my pulse spikes a split second before he slaps my pussy lips, hard. I yelp, and he spanks me again, and again.

"Yes, punished," he says, then he reaches for my ass and pinches it before he taps his hand against the plug. I hiss, but he ignores me. "Lay here while I get my tools," he says.

I shudder, wondering what he'll bring. What sort of tools do they use on an exam table?

What am I doing here? But when he comes back he just has a thin leather flogger in his hand, and what looks like a plastic rod. I cringe looking at them but at the very same time, I feel arousal coat my thighs. This is completely out of my control, and I fucking love that.

Trust him, I remind myself. *Live in the moment.*

"Close your eyes, Chandra," he instructs, his

voice so deep but soft, it reassures me. I obey. "You don't open them unless I instruct you."

I feel him circling me again, then I jump when the soft tickle of the flogger hits my thigh. "Lie still, and let me examine you," he orders, his voice as sharp as the pain he inflicts. The flogger kisses my thigh, a flurry of tingling smacks that sting and burn but quickly fade to warmth. My instinct is to fold my arms across my chest and cover my private parts, but I can't when I'm restrained like this. I shiver, my skin flaming hot and sensitized with the licks of the flogger's tongue.

Then he stops. I catch my breath. I need more. My thighs quiver and my pussy clenches. I need him to touch me.

I gasp when something cool probes my thighs.

"Open," he instructs, underscoring his command with a smack that whooshes through the air and lands on my inner thighs. I yelp when he strikes me again and again. I imagine welts rising along the tender skin of my thighs and want to clench my legs together to protect myself. My heartbeat thunders in my chest, my breath caught in my throat.

"Axle," I whisper, pleading, but my words fall on deaf ears. I'm not sure I like this.

But then the pain is gone, and his woodsy, masculine scent fills me. His heat tingles along my skin, his mouth at my ear. "Open."

Trembling, I part my legs. I'm so on edge I can't control the shaking, but then his strong, rough hands are at my knees, holding me. "Good girl," he tells me. "Let me kiss it better."

His mouth is at the bruised and swollen flesh at my thighs.

"I wanted to push you to safeword," he confesses, a note of regret in his voice. "But you won't, will you?"

"No," I whisper. My throat tightens. I want to open my eyes, but I want to obey him even more. "Why would I ever need to safeword with you?"

"I'm not safe, Chandra." He brushes my thighs with his lips, soft and sweet, and my head falls back, my eyes squeezing closed tighter. I'm growing accustomed to the low throb between my thighs, and pulse of need. I'm riding it like a high. I can control this. I can take this. I'm strong, and I can do this.

When he suckles the skin at my thighs, I arch my back. I let out an involuntary whimper, and my mind flashes to our first time together. I remember.

We're in his bed, sheets of pristine white tangled around our bodies, and he holds me as if he doesn't want me to fly away, so close our sweat-slicked skin melds together as one. He's trembling himself, exercising restraint like a bridled stallion. I can feel the way he wants to claim me with savage, hard thrusts. But it's my first time, and he doesn't want to hurt me.

He took his time ravishing my body, kissing every inch of me until my whole body teemed with need, working his way down with flutters of adoration from my temple to my toes. There isn't a place on my body that hasn't been blessed with his mouth, not a place he hasn't worshipped with his

me, the sudden ʋ·ᵤᵣ
virgin and sex scares me, but ɴʋ·
parched earth needs rain. I'll wither and die unш ..
me his. Though they would damn us to hell, every single one
of them, my heart knows better. My heart knows the truth.

This is right. This is perfect.

"I'll be as gentle as I can," he whispers in my ear, the deep, tender voice making tears spring to my eyes.

"Not too gentle," I whisper, a joke and a plea that makes him chuckle.

"I love you," he whispers, as he glides into me. My chest expands with the words and motion, and I clasp my arms around his broad, muscled back.

"I love you," I whisper, a delicious friction fusing our bodies together.

"Chandra," he says. "Open your eyes."

I blink. I forgot for a moment where I was and what we were doing. He's over me, caging me beneath him, his fierce eyes probing mine.

"You're crying."

I am?

And then I'm no longer restrained and he's pulling me to a sitting position. His gaze hardens. "You should have safeworded," he chides. "You should've goddamned safeworded. I told you to safeword if you needed to."

"I didn't want to," I say. I need to pull away from him.

"But you're overwhelmed," he says. He stands

and drags tortured fingers through his hair, clenching his jaw and pacing in front of me. "You need to learn to safeword." He pauses his pacing and points a finger at me. "I should punish you for that."

"Wait, what?" I say, swiping at my eyes. "How does that make sense?"

"Yeah," he says. "You need to learn how to do this right."

"Oh, shut up," I tell him. I'm suddenly furious. "It wasn't the pain that made me cry, and I'm sorry I did if you're gonna be a douchebag about it."

His brows shoot up so high it's almost amusing before they furrow in an angry glare.

"Well this isn't the little Chandra I knew."

"You needed to scene with me to see that?"

"You stop now," he says and damn him, he's sexy when he's all stern, with the darkened eyes and firm clench of his jaw. "You watch your tone, little girl." Even when we were younger, he never allowed me to talk back.

Hell, I loved it, though, and sometimes would get mouthy just to poke the bear. Just to feel his strength.

But I'm angry now. I was on the cusp of coming, and everything I know about sex leads me to believe it would've been freaking *epic,* but instead, I shed one little tear and now he's all mad and lecturing me and telling me I should have safeworded.

"I wasn't crying because I hurt, okay?"

He gives me a quizzical look, his lips turned down. "Then why were you crying?"

"I remembered our first time," I say. My voice drops to a whisper. "The night I gave you my virginity."

He tears his eyes from me and sighs.

"This was a mistake," he says. "We shouldn't have done this."

"Don't you dare."

He whips his head to me and his eyes narrow. "And don't you dare tell me not to dare."

I can't help it. I burst out laughing. With a shake of his head, his own eyes crinkle around the edges and he stalks back to me. Reaching for a tendril of my hair, he wraps it around his finger and tugs.

"I can tell it's been *way* too long since you've been spanked."

"Um, you spanked me like five minutes ago?"

He rolls his eyes. "I know. I mean, you've gone too long without someone taking you in hand. Not today. Just in general. You need a firm hand."

That sends a sweet little shiver through me. "Oh?"

"You could use it."

I shrug. "Maybe I could."

We sit in silence and he takes my hand.

"Are we done, then? Is this *you* safewording?"

His eyes flash at me and he squeezes my hands. "A dom doesn't safeword, honey."

"No. But a dom ends a scene and that's the same thing, isn't it?"

"No."

He says nothing else.

I blow out a breath in frustration.

"You know, I'm sitting here so damn turned on a breath of fresh air would make me come, and you're just gonna stand there?"

"We're taking a break," he says.

"Wait, what?"

He gets to his feet. "You're not behaving yourself, and naughty little girls don't get to come." Reaching down with a frown, he removes my plug. I flush and squirm, it feels so weird, and it definitely stokes my need. Then he's cleaning me. "Up you go."

No one makes me angrier than Noah. But no one is more fierce, more powerful, more determined, and I love that.

God, I wish I didn't.

Tugging me along with him, we walk toward doorway. "Come with me and behave, and I'll consider letting you climax later."

I'm still frustrated and can't help but mutter, "will just do the damn job myself if you won't let me."

Turning to face me, he captures my jaw in one of his huge hands. His fingers are rough and calloused, and I feel his correction right between my thighs. My eyes are riveted to his.

"You will not. You agreed to scene with me today, so that sweet little cunt of yours belongs to me unless you safeword. You safeword, and this ends. You touch yourself without permission, and I'll whip your ass."

"Ooh," I say, because I need to make a snarky

comment as my heart slams in my chest and he's turning me on again. "Naughty."

He rolls his eyes heavenward before he slaps my ass good and hard. I'm still bare and still sore, so I come up on my toes and squeal. Ignoring my protest, he takes me by the hand and leads me to the door.

"You see that wall of tools?" he asks.

"Mhm." My body's a live wire of need, and a mere glance makes me want to bend right back over the bench.

"Keep them in mind, little girl."

I war with arousal and curiosity and anger as we exit the dungeon and walk toward his private room. It's cooler out here, and I shiver, so he pulls me a little closer with an arm around me. He pulls out his cell phone, hits a button, and slides it up to his ear. After a moment of listening, he pockets the phone.

"Blizzard warning still in effect," he says.

"Damn. I wanted to order pizza."

He huffs out a mirthless laugh. "After a good dinner one can forgive anybody," he says. It's a quote, but I can't remember from where.

"I'm rusty," I tell him, shooting him a quizzical look, and the stern facade cracks for a second when his lips twitch.

"Oscar Wilde."

He gestures for me to come into his room, and I do. I should feel weird, freshly spanked and aroused and naked, and I'm not quite sure why I don't. I kinda love this.

"Bed," he says, snapping his fingers.

I bite back a retort. I want to scene with him. But I asked for this, so I'll give it to him.

I lay down in the bed, and I have to admit, this feels good. I'm tired after all that, totally exhausted. Closing my legs is mildly arousing, but those scenes took the wind right out of me. The heaviness of sleep settles onto me like a weighted blanket, and my eyes go half-lidded.

"Alright, I'm getting us food. You stay right there and rest," he says. And before I can ask him what he's going to get, he's gone. I listen hard, curious if he's going outside in this weather, but there's no way he's doing that.

The door clicks shut behind him and I'm left alone on his bed. Lying here under the sheets and blankets, I'm not sure what to do with myself. Why am I even here? His lingering scent clings to the cool, soft sheets, to the heavy blanket over me, and hell, it permeates the whole room. I squirm on the blankets, so tempted to slide my fingers through my folds and take care of business. I'm swollen and needy. But he'll punish me if I do.

To distract myself, I pick up my phone and check my messages. There's one from Marla.

Marla: Hey, everything okay? How are you?

I feel a little guilty not telling her everything. After all, she's a member here, too, and she knows Axle well. Should I tell her I'm here? I decide against it, because I have no idea exactly what I'm going to tell her. *Oh, hey, met up with the guy I knew years ago who I was in love with and we decided, just for the hell of it, to have a no-holds-barred day of kinky sex. And you?*

I shake my head and keep it generic.

I'm good. How are you?

Marla: Okay. No, I'm kinda fantastic. I wanted to meet up again at the club tonight, but the website says they're closed. Maybe next week?

Yes, sounds good to me. But girl, I want all the details. You're just going to say you're kind of fantastic?

Marla: I went home with Viktor last night. His private dungeon makes Verge look like the kiddie gym.

I grin to myself. This is awesome. Even though I'm excited for her, I'm a little scared. Does she even know who he is?

Is he a good guy, though? Like how well do you know him?

The door to the room opens, and Axle walks in carrying a tray with a bunch of food. I feel a little guilty holding my phone, though I'm not really sure why. He didn't tell me I couldn't have my phone, but I have this weird idea I should be submissively lying there or something. I put it down.

"Do you know who Viktor is?" I ask him.

He draws his brows together. "The name's familiar," he says. "Why?"

I don't want to rat out my friend, but at the same time, I want to know details.

"Marla left with him last night," I say. "She

texted and says she's excited, but I'm not really sure how well she knows him."

He slides the tray on the bedside table. There are two turkey sandwiches and some chips.

"Well, Marla's a big girl," he says. "She knows better than to give too much trust too soon to a guy she doesn't know, doesn't she?"

I look down at my naked body and back up at him, and it seems he reads my mind, because he clucks his tongue. "Afraid you're the pot calling the kettle black?"

I shake my head. "You're hardly a guy I don't know," I tell him.

"Not sure that's true, babe," he says, handing me a sandwich. I don't even ask him where he got it or how. I'm starving, and I know he's only going to give me something good to eat. I take a bite, chew and swallow, and don't say anything at first. So many questions. But where to begin?

"Why do you say that?" I finally ask. I take another bite of sandwich and watch him as he chews and swallows before he swigs down half a bottle of water.

"The man you knew was a good man," he says. "Preached the good word to people. Helped people choose between right and wrong. Counseled them. Performed sacraments with hands blessed and sanctified to do so. But I was corrupt. I shouldn't have been a priest to begin with."

I swallow my own water and sit up in bed. "Is anyone really *good*?" I ask.

He shakes his head. "Sure they are. And don't downplay the shit I've done."

"The Noah I knew was a strong man," I say quietly. My voice is a bit shaky, but I press on. "He made mistakes. And yes, he never should have joined the priesthood to begin with. But he did the right thing and when he knew he'd made a mistake, he left that life behind, because it was never his to begin with."

He smiles sadly. "But we were talking about Marla."

I smile back. "And now we're talking about you."

"I shouldn't let you take control here," he says.

"I'm naked in your bed, dying to climax, and welted and red all over from your hand. What part of this am I controlling?"

He tugs a strand of my hair playfully. "Adorable," he says. "And yeah, that's why I left. I didn't maintain my vow of celibacy, and I couldn't pretend to be someone I wasn't."

"I couldn't, either." I speak so softly at first, I wonder if he heard me, because he doesn't react, just opens a bag of chips and pops one in his mouth. But after a minute, he speaks up again.

"Sometimes growing up means making mistakes, learning from them, and doing better with the next choices we have. You left your home. You went off and pursued your dreams. Nothing wrong with that."

"And there's nothing wrong with choosing to live the way you do," I tell him. "You could have stayed, like how many others who stay, and keep mistresses and lovers? But you didn't. You recognized you weren't meant to choose that life, and you went to pursue your own."

He nods, thoughtfully. "Back to Marla," he finally says, and I know he's choosing to change the subject on purpose.

I hope he's at least thinking about what I said to him.

"Marla," I repeat.

"Keep in touch with her," he says. "She'll do the right thing, but sometimes people need the space to do that."

The irony kills me. "Maybe you should take your own advice," I say, but his demeanor changes and his gaze turns stern. My belly flips when the low tone of his voice arrests me. "That's enough now, Chandra. I've let you speak freely. Now this conversation is over." He raises a brow and gestures to the tray. "Eat."

I bite back a retort and take another bite. It tastes good, and as the food settles in my belly, my grumpiness begins to abate.

"Damn," I mutter to myself. "Guess I was a little hangry."

"A little?" he asks. He leans down and gathers up the empty tray. "Now," he says, walking to the door. "You take a nap. When you wake up, we'll continue where we left off."

Nap? I don't nap. I do things. Although I don't say anything, he gives me a look that dares me to defy him and a little part of me wants to, but my ass still stings, and my eyes do feel really heavy.

"Fine," I say. I lay back on the bed and let the food settle in my belly. I try to clear my mind, but it's a jumble of thoughts and confusion. I wish I could clear it. My mind begins to wander as he goes about the room and leaves me to rest. I close my eyes, and a memory assaults my mind like a blow.

I'm alone, clutching my abdomen in pain and rocking back and forth. I can't share my agony with anyone. I hate blood, and there's so much blood. I flushed the toilet and flushed again, and again, even when the water ran clear, because I needed to know everything was gone.

Everything. It's all gone.

I feared my parents would find the positive pregnancy test and I made up my mind then and there it was time for me to move out.

The local paper has finally stopped calling me. Rumors are beginning to die down. Sometimes when I go out, little old ladies at the supermarket still whisper behind their fingers, but mostly people have begun to move on.

"Father Noah" is but a distant memory now. He's turned in his collar and moved on. I told him to. I begged him to. But I can't bring myself to forgive him for actually doing it.

We were careless. So careless. I never should have let him near me. The second he touched me, my self-control began to wane. But I gave him my heart first. He listened to me. He laughed with me. He cared. And I fell in love.

He wasn't mine to have, though. And as I stand here and wash my hands over and over again, I know, this is the curse sent to me from above. He wasn't mine to have and neither was this baby. Both have been ripped painfully from me, tearing my heart into pieces that will never mend.

A knock sounds on the door. "I'll be right out," I shout, my voice unnaturally high.

"You've been in there a long time," my mother snaps. She knows something is wrong, and she'll never forgive me for the scrutiny and scorn I dragged them through.

"I'm almost done," I say, my voice gaining an edge. I look at myself in the mirror. There are bags under the dark brown eyes rimmed in red. My face is thinner. I've lost weight. My hair hangs in crazy waves around my face, unkempt and unruly.

I splash water on my face and make myself stare at my stained hands, then grab my abdomen when another spasm of pain contracts. I hiss out breath, trying to regain my composure.

"Chandra!" Her fist pounds on the door.

"I have my period!" I shout, my shrill tone stopping her. "Leave me alone!"

She says nothing, but I hear her walk away, and a part of me silently begs for her to come back. I want someone to hold me. Someone to tell me I'm not evil, that I didn't bring this curse down on me.

But there is no one. The only person who ever believed in me is gone.

"Chandra?"

I wake with a start and clutch the blanket to my chest. I blink, trying to remember where I am. God, I so have to get my act together.

"You alright?" He sits beside the bed, his brow drawn in consternation.

"Yeah," I whisper. "I'm sorry, I must've fallen asleep. I was having a bad dream."

"S'alright," he says, and he gives my shoulder a little squeeze. "I have good news."

"Do you?" I sit up and try to mentally shove the weight that settled on my chest off, but it's leaden and immovable. I'll have to let it seep off me.

"Yeah," he says. "The forecast says the snow is over. It's turning to rain now. Looks like you'll be able to go home soon."

My heart sinks, deflated. That isn't good news at all. It's terrible news.

"Oh," I say, looking away.

How can I leave him? I feel like our session's barely begun and it's already over.

"I can leave soon?" I ask. I can't bring myself to say it but only repeat it incredulously. I tear myself away from his stern, tender eyes, his beautiful, powerful body, the hands that can be so harsh yet so tender. There's an ache in my chest. I don't want to leave him. I've buried a part of me that was complete when I'm with him and now he's ripping me away again.

"C'mere," he says gruffly. He tugs me onto his lap. "Never could stand to see you sad."

"I'm not sad," I protest, but it's a lie. I'm devastated.

"You were a minute ago." I lean into his strong embrace. He smells so damn good. I let myself be held, and I nuzzle my cheek against the softness of his shirt. When I'm quiet, I can hear his heartbeat. "Can you tell me what the bad dream was?"

I want to. God, I want to. It was his baby, too, and he deserves to know the truth.

But I can't. Not now. Tonight, I'll go home, and I'm not sure if I'll ever see him again. Telling him about the baby will bring back a connection neither one of us is ready for and memories I'm not ready to face. We can't do it. Not now. Maybe not ever.

I shake my head. "Alright, then, babe," he says. His grip tightens.

"So," I say, needing to lighten the mood. "Are you staying here tonight?"

"Maybe. Thinking about it. I want to be here in case anyone comes. We're closed, but I think it's probably for the best." He shrugs. "My place is boring anyway."

"Oh." Suddenly, my need to get home isn't so strong as it was before. "Axle?" It feels weird calling him that, but it's growing on me.

"Yeah?" The rumble of his voice travels over my skin, and I pull a little closer.

"Can we finish this session?"

His laugh is like the low beat of a bass drum, rhythmic, soothing, and a little intimidating and I flush pink.

"Finish as in, you need to climax?"

My mouth goes dry, and I'm suddenly super embarrassed. "I didn't say—"

"Yeah, babe," he interrupts. "We can finish." Releasing me, he points to a corner of his room and orders in a sharp command. "Go kneel and wait for me."

Wait for me.

Why does that make my pulse spike? And I

can't believe I'm still completely naked in front of him. This is *crazy*.

I jump when his palm cracks against my ass, reigniting my need. "Ow!"

"You say '*yes, sir.*'"

I rub my stinging ass with a little pout. "Yes, sir."

I go to the corner of the room that's dark in shadow and notice a little bookshelf and armchair I didn't see before. This is almost like a little sitting room. Glancing quickly at the bookshelf, it doesn't surprise me the titles are non-fiction and spiritual. This is his room, after all.

I kneel as he's instructed me, my head bowed, so fully conscious of his eyes on me. I take a deep breath in and release it, doing what he told me to before. Letting it all out.

A flash of my memory comes to me again, but I shove it away. No. That was in the past. All of it was. I'm here now researching my book in the most visceral way possible. Right. That's it.

He prowls behind me, tapping something against his palm.

"In position."

My spine goes ramrod straight but I keep my head bowed and my hands in my lap.

Something cool trails along my naked ass, but the sound of metal on metal makes me freeze. My breath freezes in my lungs. My chest constricts. My pulse races like thundering hooves. What is that sound behind me? He likes keeping me in a state of suspense like this.

I consciously let out a breath. Hell, maybe I like it, too.

This. This is what I need.

I shiver when he slides something around my neck, then clicks it in place, but I know that if I move my head, he'll spank me with whatever's tapping on his palm. When he tugs, I feel what's on my neck. He's collared and chained me.

"Just like that," he says. "Hold your chain." He places the length in my hand but doesn't walk away. When he brushes something along my inner thigh, a little shudder courses through me.

"Sir?"

"Relax, Chandra," he says. "Part your legs."

Holding my chain, I do as he says and part my legs, shaking a little. "Good girl. Just like that."

Something smooth and cool is gliding along my folds. I close my eyes. It's so personal, so private, but I'm still primed from being aroused before. I whimper and try to maintain my position. He's positioning something over my swollen, throbbing parts.

"Keep this here," he says, taking my hand and positioning it over the device in my hand that vibrates and hums. To my shock, it suckles my clit and I convulse with the power of it.

"Oh my God."

"Quiet, Chandra," he commands. "Be a good girl now."

"Yes, sir," I whisper. I'm holding the thing in place when he tugs my collar, and my eyes fly open. The little machine in my hand sucks and vibrates and I whimper, grinding my hips. It feels so damn good but it's so intense.

"Sir?" my voice is hoarse, choked.

Lifting my chin in his hand, he tips my eyes to his to maintain my gaze. "You're allowed to come when you're ready," he says. With his free hand he wraps the chain tightly around his fingers and gives a little tug. For a brief second, it restricts my air like his hand on me. I gasp, but he lets the chain go.

My pussy throbs, faster, harder. I'm going to climax. The suck and whir at my clit continues with relentless pulsation, and then I'm soaring, my thighs contracting as my pussy clenches and my sex convulses. I try to scream but his grip on the chain at my neck is too much. I have to consciously work hard at not looking away from him, because my eyes want to close and ride this high.

I drop the tool, and yet my hips still convulse violently. I'm half-crying, half-moaning, as my climax rips through me like lightning, hard and fast and blinding. My voice is hoarse. It's all I can do to maintain my position. He's not touching me, nothing is, and yet I'm still climaxing, still contracting and writhing. It's too much. Too intense.

"Axle," I whisper. I'm lightheaded from the chain at my neck, whimpering. Then he's kneeling beside me and his hand is at my pussy. I moan when he presses his fingers between my legs. I'm too sensitive. The slightest touch of his finger makes my whole lower body shudder.

"Might've been too much," he says. He unsnaps the chain and coils it on the floor.

"Wh—what was that?" I ask. He soothes my rocking hips by placing one palm on my abdomen and the other on my lower back, holding me still.

"Sonic clit stim," he says.

"That was g-good," I tell him. My teeth are chattering. I don't want to wimp out, but I can't control the shivers and shudders.

"I'm glad," he says. "Still, you may need to be eased into this. Come on. Stand, now." I get to my feet and turn to face him. "Good," he says. It strikes me that he's still the same Noah he was back then, taking such careful care of me, but I have to banish the thought. "Chandra," he says, an air of finality in his voice that makes me pay attention. "I'm calling this day off for now. You've had a good taste of a few things, but you're done for now."

I don't argue. I know by the look he's giving me now that he's made up his mind. There's no use trying to talk him into something once he has and part of me knows he's right. I *am* done. Still, I'm disappointed when he leads me back to the bed. My legs shake, my hands tremble.

"Damn, I didn't know it would hit you that hard."

"I'm a d-delicate flower," I stammer, trying to make light of the situation but I'm shivering violently, and I can't make it stop.

"Baby," he says, and the soft tone of his voice makes tears sting my eyes. I can't handle this intensity. I need to get away. Sitting on the edge of bed, he draws me onto his lap. "Delicate flower," he repeats. "I don't think so."

"I a-am."

"You're a goddamn cactus."

That makes me giggle. We sit in silence for a while. I listen to the sound of his heart beating and try to get my mind to rest, to stop racing, but it's not an easy task. I inhale his strong, masculine scent and letting my fingers rest on his chest, letting myself wish that this was real and not make believe. My hips still quiver a little, and I want it to stop, but I can't control the tremors that still shudder through me. Placing his hand on my lower back, he pulls my torso against his.

I like the feel of his hand on me so much more than the things he's used.

Several minutes pass while he just holds me and helps me adjust to coming down. "Well, that was all noted for the next book," I mutter. "You do have a devious mind sometimes, don't you?"

"Not sometimes. All the time. You better now?"

"I think so."

"Okay, then let's get you dressed and home."

My stomach drops. "Maybe I'm not better," I amend. "Maybe my stomach hurts a little."

He reaches for my chin and lifts my gaze up. "I want the truth, Chandra."

He can't have the truth. Not now. I can't bring myself to say all the things I want to. But it turns out I don't have to.

"Give me a mask," I whisper, the first words of

an Oscar Wilde quote that's come to me out of nowhere.

"And I'll tell you the truth," he finishes. He shakes his head at me. "You won't quote yourself out of this one. There are no masks. Now tell me."

"Honestly?" my voice comes out on a shaky whisper. "I forgot what we were talking about." And I have. Staring into those eyes that once loved me, I forgive him. It's a baptism by fire. I've been thrown into this pit and scourged clean of what plagued me. My love of Noah has never left me; I loved him then and I love him now. It's myself that I blamed, under the guise of blaming him. But here, stripped down and exposed, I'm once more the girl who loved him. I can't remember what we were talking about. I can't remember why I was angry at him. And when he bends down and touches his lips to mine, I forget my own name.

Our breath mingles, my body rises, and I wrap my hands around the strong column of his neck while he holds me. The world around me darkens as I submerge fully into him. I'm drowning but not afraid, for this little death slays the last of my fears. With his mouth on mine, I'm his again. Maybe I never stopped being his. He kisses me with the tenderness and desperation of a long-lost lover. I'm breathless, boneless, and utterly his. When he pulls his mouth off mine I whisper a tortured, "Noah."

"Chandra," he whispers back, turning to lay me gently on the bed. "We can't do this."

"Why not?" I ask him, angry and desperate, but when I meet his eyes, I don't see the tortured man I expect, but instead that look of firm decision I'm so familiar with.

He takes my hand and squeezes. "I want to take you right now. I want to make love to you until you can't remember your own name and fuck you until you scream mine."

"Then do it," I say, already knowing my plea will fall on deaf ears. Once he's made up his mind, there's no turning back.

"Not now," he says. A muscle in his jaw twitches. "You're not in your right frame of mind. I'd be taking advantage."

Who is he to say what frame of mind I'm in? Like a silly, spoiled child, I grab the pillow off the bed and whip it at him, but he catches it before it hits him and places it back on the bed.

"Enough, Chandra." He raises one finger in warning. "You behave yourself."

I bite my lip. Throwing a tantrum never got me my way with him and it won't now. Anyway, I'm better than that.

"Mad," I whisper. He isn't even touching me, but I need to safeword. It's too late, though. He's already ended the scene, and I'm just grappling for control he won't give me.

"Good girl." He tugs a lock of my hair and despite my frustration, I smile a little. I still like being his good girl. "Get yourself dressed, and I'll take you home."

He walks out of the room. It isn't until he's gone that I notice my clothes lie next to the bed, neatly folded and ready for me to wear. He must have brought them in while I was sleeping. I dress with trembling fingers. Dressing feels like a failure somehow, like I didn't pass the test. Was there a test?

Even though I don't want this to end, I wonder if he has a point. I folded like a house of cards when he kicked the kink level up a notch. Maybe I *do* need to be eased into this. I'm still not exactly sure what happened here.

He called this scene to an end. Or did I?

But this isn't over.

Chapter Ten

Axle

While she dresses, I make one more round through Verge, making sure that everything's secured. I considered staying here, but it's time to get her home, and I want to be sure she gets there safely.

The real reason I'm making one last visit through the club is because I need to get a handle on myself, and I can't be near her right now. I'm so fucking hard it hurts to walk, but it's more than that. I'm an addict in withdrawal who can't be satisfied until I give into my craving. But not like this. Not when she's stripped and bared and drunk on submission. I need to know when I take her again that she's fully consenting and not under duress.

It felt good to play with her. To have her at my mercy. Chandra's the most beautiful woman I've ever laid eyes on, it makes my cock throb just thinking about how it felt inflicting pain on her willing body. The cuffs and flogger were good in their own right, but I liked when I actually touched her. My mouth is branded with the taste of her skin, my senses filled with the scent of her arousal. I slam the door to the breakroom harder than necessary, take out my phone, and dial Tobias.

"Hey."

"How are things going?" I ask.

"Good. Chad had the day off from school, Diana's working from home, and we're taking it slow. You?"

"Good," I tell him. "But it's time I get…" I pause. How much do I tell him? "I gotta get my guest home. Looks like the snow's dying down."

"Sounds good. Later, fill me in about that guest of yours?"

My jaw ticks as I stare at the wall. If I tell him no, he'll respect that and won't ask again.

"Yeah. But when the time is right, okay? She's an old flame and I'm not sure where this is going yet."

"Of course," he says. "Thanks for everything. I'll stay closed tonight, but we'll open back up again tomorrow. Sound good?"

"I'm there."

I disconnect the call and turn to see Chandra in the doorway. She's dressed in the clothes from the night before, her hair slightly disheveled. She wears no make-up or jewelry, but her hair shines and her face glows, and she looks like an angel.

"Old flame?" she asks. "What is this, 1950?"

I take her hand and swat her pretty ass. "Yep. Walking out of here with a bonafide throwback, babe. You game?"

She shrugs. "We'll see." She's subdued now and lost the saucy brattiness she got when she tossed the pillow at me. I'm a little disappointed. Though I want her submission, I like the little vixen in her. Still, I won't let her act out to get what she wants. I'll give her space to really figure that out and right now, she needs time.

I get our coats and we pull them on.

"Where to?" I ask. God, this is killing me. It feels like there are too many layers between us now, too much padding. My balls are heavy and aching, my cock tight and swollen. I want to scene with her to completion... again, and again, and again.

More than that, though, I don't want to let her go, back into the wide, wide world, with no one to protect her. No one to make sure she's safe. No way of knowing she'll come back to me.

"Oh, I'll just get a cab," she says, gesturing at the big black entryway door.

Oh *hell no*, we're not playing that game.

I shake my head. "I'm going with you. Cab it is. Address?"

Her lips pull down in a frown. "Alright, then," she finally says. "But you're not coming up."

"I wouldn't ask," I tell her. "And that's fine."

She looks to me expectantly like she expects me to argue the point, but I'm not playing any games with her. I jumped in too fast, too soon.

Under the guise of helping her, I pursued my own selfish needs. What we had once is gone, and we aren't the people we once were. Will we ever be the same?

It's freezing cold outside. Her breath comes in billowy clouds, and I can't help myself. I make sure she's good and warm, with her jacket pulled snugly around her. The snow's plowed on the street and sidewalks but stands in large drifts on both sides of the streets. It's surreal, too quiet here while we're surrounded by snow. We hail down a cab, I open the door and gesture for her to get in, then I slide in beside her. She gives the driver her address.

We sit in silence as he drives toward her home, until I finally break it.

"I never expected seeing you at Verge," I tell her.

"Mmm," is all she says.

I need to know if she's coming back. "Are you planning on returning?"

"Definitely." She's looking out her window and tapping her fingers on her knee.

Definitely? She's coming back, but she hasn't made plans with me. If she comes back here and hooks up with another dom—

"When is that?" I can't keep the bite out of my tone.

Frowning, she looks my way. "When I decide to."

God, I want to put her over my lap and spank that sass right out of her, to make her open up again, but it's not my privilege and I can't dom her into trusting me. I need to earn that privilege.

"Is that right?" I ask, trying to keep my tone even, but failing. I sound like a cockblocked teen.

"Yeah," she says.

I blow out a breath. "You're not scening with another dom."

Her mouth drops open and she stares at me before she speaks. "So let me get this straight," she says. "*You* won't touch me, yet you won't allow another dom to?"

"Who said I wouldn't touch you?" I ask. "Sweetheart, I did a hell of a lot more than *touch* you."

Her cheeks flame and she turns to looks out the window. She mutters something under her breath, but I don't catch it.

"What's that?"

"Nothing."

God, I should have spanked her harder.

"*Chandra.*"

"I said *yes, you did.*" She sighs.

"Okay, fine," I tell her. "Let's compromise."

Pursing her lips, she raises a brow to me and crosses her arms on her chest. Yeah, I definitely could've plied that flogger a little better.

"Yeah? What's your compromise?"

"If you want to come to the club and scene, you call me. I'll be your dom for the night. But we don't kiss, and we definitely don't fuck."

She huffs out a breath and rolls her eyes, but her cheeks are a little pink.

"I'll think about it," she says.

The cab pulls to a stop outside a tall building with mirrored windows. "Your place?" I ask.

She nods and hesitates.

I want to leave with her. Go upstairs. Jesus, I want to. But I don't trust myself. And I know she needs distance from me. Still, I have to see her in safely.

"I'll take you in to make sure you're safe, but then I have to head home myself."

She starts to hand money to the driver, but I pull it back and pay him myself.

We exit the cab. I want to take her hand but there's this air between us, a wall I can't take down, not yet. She's angry at me and she has a right to be. I took advantage today. I did it under the guise of giving her what she needed, but I know better.

"Nice place," I say.

Jesus. *Lame.*

I shove my hands in my pockets as we ride the elevator to the fifth floor.

"Thank you," she says absentmindedly. "My mom would lose her mind."

She would. She always wanted her daughter to live in opulence, unscathed by the common people.

"She would, but that doesn't matter." I ignore how she relaxes a little when I say that, like she needed permission to not give a shit. "How long have you been here?" The elevator swoops upward.

"A year. Where do you live?"

"I have a one-bedroom apartment not far from

131

Verge," I tell her. "Takes fifteen minutes by taxi, but it's not far from the repair shop and I spend most nights in the private room anyway."

"It's like your bunker."

"You could say that."

"Tell me about the shop?"

We talk about our jobs for a minute, but then we're at her floor.

"So I'm… okay now," she says. "You can go now… Axle."

I don't want to leave her. There's a tugging in my gut that tells me to stay, that she needs me tonight. I put her through hell today, and I don't like leaving her alone. I've split her open and now I'm leaving her, raw and exposed.

"You sure you're okay?" I ask. "We went through a lot today."

She blinks and looks away. "I'm good," she says to her shoes. "I want to get some sleep tonight. I have work early tomorrow morning."

I nod. I have to respect that she hasn't invited me in, and she wants some time to herself. What the hell's wrong with me? I went seven years without seeing her and now the thought of one night makes me clench my fists.

She opens her door and stands tentatively in the doorway. "Good night," she says. This is wrong. God, this is so damn wrong.

Fuck this.

I lean in, grab a fistful of her thick, fragrant hair, and yank her head back. When her mouth falls open I capture it with a kiss that tells her that I don't care if seven minutes or seven years has passed, I own this mouth. Her palm is pressed up against my chest. She doesn't push me away but fists my shirt, clenching it between taut fingers. When she has a good, firm grip, she tugs me closer to her.

Hell no.

Without thinking, I wrap my hand around her wrists, removing her grip on me, and backpedal her until she's flush against the doorframe. I pin both arms to her sides and glide my tongue against hers, a silent command to surrender. She melts against me and submits to my mouth.

She'll submit to all of me.

In time.

She leans in for more, my cue to pull apart and leave her with the memory of what she wants.

"Sleep well," I whisper in her ear. Her cheeks are flushed, her pupils dilated, and it takes all my self-control to walk away from her and not push her back into that apartment and claim her hard and fast up against the door.

I will.

She nods, then turns away, shutting the door behind her. I wait until I hear the click of locks fastening before I leave, and then I remember.

I don't even have her cell phone number. *God.*

Guess I'll be paying a visit to Marla's bright and early tomorrow morning.

I wake up the next morning early, with Chandra on my mind, so fucking hard I throw the sheets down and hit the shower before I can lay in bed and dwell. I'm too much of the good Catholic boy to rub one off in the shower. It's a point of pride with me. I'm stronger than my most base urges, and I don't fuck around. I welcome the discomfort so I can stay focused.

Today's my day off from my day job. Marla put in a special order for me, and I told her I'd pick that up on my day off.

And Chandra will be there.

After getting dressed and grabbing a quick breakfast, I check my phone. I've got four messages. I sit at the bar in my kitchen, sipping coffee, and read a message from Tobias.

Tobias: Snow's cleared. See you tonight?

Hell yes.

A second message is from Zack.

Zack: Morning. Tobias called me, says there's concerning footage on the security feed from the night you were on as DM. Talk tonight?

I'll be there.

But when I go to put my phone down, a message flashes across the screen from a number I don't recognize.

Hi. Marla gave me your number. It's Chandra.

My heartbeat quickens like a teenager's, but I keep my shit together and reply.

Morning, Chandra. Did you sleep well?

Chandra: Yes, thank you. You?

I smirk at the phone. I slept like shit, tossing and turning with thoughts of her and our past, and woke this morning with morning wood so hard I could've cracked diamonds with it.

Yeah, it was alright. Heading to work soon?

Chandra: Yes. Hey, I just wanted to thank you for yesterday.

Thank me? What the hell is she talking about?

You don't have anything to thank me for, but you're welcome.

Chandra: Do you still drink your coffee black with two sugars?

I smile.

Yeah.

Chandra: Come meet me early at the shop, and I'll make you a cup?

I grin.

See you soon.

I toss my cup in the sink, grab a coat, and head out the door before I even think about what I'm doing, and almost collide into a little ball of blonde-haired, blue-eyed energy standing right outside the door.

"Good morning, Mr. Rivet." Kylie, the kindergartner next door, pirouettes right in front of me and nearly topples over with the weight of her bag.

"Kylie! Leave Mr. Rivet alone. You shouldn't be doing your dance moves in the hallway. Wait until we're outside." Kylie's mom Abigail corrects her. I give Abigail a smile to let her know it's fine. Her mouse brown hair is pulled back into a thick braid, and she's already dressed in her waitress uniform. She smiles back.

"Nah, she's fine, Abigail. How are you?" I lock the door and pocket the key before turning to face them.

Leaning in to zip her daughter's coat, she says, "Oh, I'm good."

"Mama has a date tonight!" the little girl chirps.

"Hush, Kylie." But Abigail's cheek flush. She's a pretty, young woman I've known for a few years now, since her daughter was only a toddler.

"Oh?"

"It's nothing," she says with a wave of her hand, but then her attention is drawn back to her daughter, who pirouettes so hard she crashes into me. I catch Kylie and right her.

"Kylie!"

I shake my head with a chuckle. "I haven't had my coffee yet and need to wake up." Then I give Kylie a hard look. "But maybe you ought to do what your mama says."

Kylie grins, waves, and runs out the door to the bus stop.

Abigail shakes her head before she chases after her daughter.

"Bye, Axle!"

"Have a good date," I yell after her, which earns me a groan before she leaves. There was a time when I was mildly interested in her. She's always dating someone, though, and nothing ever developed between the two of us other than friendly camaraderie, but now I grow a little wistful as I go outside and see the kids and their parents waiting for the bus. Half a dozen of them stand outside. Two of them are giggling and sharing a package of those little muffins in a bag. One is holding some kind of game thing in his hand, fingers flying, his tongue sticking out in concentration. The parents stand around, sipping coffee out of travel mugs, and I wonder.

If Chandra and I had stayed together, would we have a little girl with Chandra's bright eyes doing pirouettes in the hall? If we'd had a child back then, she or he would be about this age now, off to kindergarten or first grade. Learning to tie shoes and ride a bike, and for the first time in a really long time, the very notion pulls at my gut. I want that. A family.

We were young, and stupid, and had unprotected sex. We could've ended up just like this, raising a child together. Maybe then, we would've stayed together.

I shake my head to myself and put my head down. I never think about having kids. I never think about relationships. This is fucking with my head, and I have things to do. A gust of wind kicks up. I let the bitter cold whip at me, welcoming the sting so it clears my head.

None of that happened, so it doesn't matter. It might never. It doesn't do me a lick of good to focus on that now. I've got a girl to meet, and she's making me coffee. I need to get to know her. Reacquaint myself with her and learn who she's become. What makes her laugh, and what makes her cry. The kinds of books she writes and the kinds of books she reads. Who her friends are. What keeps her up at night and what puts a smile on her face. And how I can keep that smile there.

Chandra

I walk around the bookstore much earlier than I should be, like I'm waiting for my date to arrive. This is ridiculous. The clock hasn't even struck eight yet, and we open at nine, but I tell myself there are things I need to do to occupy myself.

It has nothing to do with needing to see him again.

I yawn hugely, my eyes watering, as I make coffee. Last night, I came home with my mind teeming with ideas for my book, and I wrote long and hard until the wee hours of the morning. Today will be a long day.

I had to do it, though. I had to capture the memory of what he did to me. How it felt. How it awakened in me the need for more. And writing my own, controlled world of love and romance quiets the inner voice that plagues me with memories of my past.

So I wrote until I fell into a short, deep sleep, more like a nap than anything, and when I woke I needed to see him.

It took a little finagling to get his number out of Marla, but eventually she caved. My hands shook as I texted, but I needed to at least make some contact.

My heart soared when he responded so quickly.

What are you doing? I mentally berate myself.

I'm acting like an impulsive girl, not the self-contained woman I've tried so hard to become. This is crazy.

The only people for me are the mad ones.

I grab a broom and sweep the floor while the comforting, fragrant scent of coffee permeates the air. The floor's immaculate, though, as Marla keeps it in pristine condition, and I'm only sweeping away imaginary dirt. My hands shake, and I need to keep myself occupied. I sweep the imaginary dirt into the dustpan and dump nothing into the trash barrel, then grab a feather duster and brush the dust-free tops of the books on display in front when the doorbell jingles and my heart nearly leaps straight out of my chest.

He's here. God, he's here, standing right in the doorway wearing a knit cap pulled down tight, blue eyes glinting at me in the early morning light. His lips quirk up and he gives me a little salute. Damn, he looks so good like that, all masculine and sexy and rugged. A delicious thrill shivers through me.

"Well aren't you a picture." The deep rumble of his voice rakes over my skin and coaxes a smile out of me.

I look down at myself on instinct. I'm wearing a burgundy sweater, black leggings that hug my curves, and knee-length leather boots. My cheeks flush.

"Thanks?"

"No question. Just thanks is good. Listen, that front walk needs a good shovel and icing. Whoever plowed it did a terrible job."

"I know," I say, "But I don't know where she keeps the shovel. I looked."

"I know where it is."

I don't like that he knows where Marla's shovel is. It feels too familiar, too domestic. I ignore the stab of jealousy that hits me in the gut and grab my coat off the hook behind the counter. "I'll help."

He raises a brow. "No, you won't. I've got this. I'll take some of that coffee when I get back in though." Shooting me a wink, he opens a little closet I never even noticed and removes a shovel and a bucket of ice melt. I don't like him going back out, and I take a step toward him, but he only shakes his head at me. It's enough to get me to stay where I am.

I forgot what it was like to be with a man who bosses me around like he does. Whose natural instincts are to protect and be chivalrous. Women say that chivalry is dead, but being around Axle, I know it's not. When I knew him before, he always carried the heavy bags, held doors open for me, pulled out chairs and made sure I stayed dry when it rained. Some would find it overbearing. I loved it. And now that he's back, I can tell he hasn't really changed. He's grown up a little, and I have, too, but he's still who he always was at the core.

I grab the duster and go to the front window, swiping at imaginary smudges before I wipe a peep hole and look out. He's hunched over, scraping at the icy snow by the entrance until he gets to bare ground, little by little removing every inch of it, then he shakes ice melt over the freshly-shoveled surface. An older man walks by, walking with tentative footsteps. Axle looks up, says something to him, then reaches for the man's elbow to steady him. He helps him until he gets his footing, then watches until the man's out of sight. My heart warms. Even when I knew him seven years ago, he was protective of everyone and anyone. It was partly why our affair was so hard on him, because he felt as if he'd let down the people he'd sworn to protect and care for. And in a way, he did.

I swallow.

It wasn't right then. We were two people, stuck in the wrong place at the wrong time, circling each other for answers but finding only empty promises.

Now will be different.

My eyes water and I swipe at them, swallowing the massive lump in my throat.

It's the scene, I tell myself. He made me so bare and raw yesterday that today I'm a mess. That's got to be it.

The door opens, and he comes in, shaking off ice and snow, his cheeks and nose red. I go to him and take his coat, then hand him a cup of coffee.

"Thank you for doing that," I tell him. "Marla will appreciate it. Come sit and have some breakfast?"

"No problem. Thanks, babe." I ignore the way my cheeks flush.

"You always were old-fashioned," I tell him. "You'd like it if I sat by the fire and knitted while you cleaned your gun, huh?"

He snorts. "I hate hunting, and you don't

knit." Taking a long pull from his coffee mug, he sighs. "This is delicious."

He doesn't deny the old-fashioned bit, though. And it doesn't bother me. I'd love sitting by him. Serving him. Being the woman he comes home to. I never could bear the thought of doing that the way my parents wanted me to, but somehow being *his*… it's different. It feels right.

I realize with a start that I'm letting my mind get away ahead of me. What the hell am I thinking about?

"Maybe go sit down and I'll bring this to you," I suggest, pulling out a tray of warm muffins.

He heads to the back of the shop where circular tables wait for customers. Pulling out a chair, he folds himself into it, and my heart hammers in my chest and my mouth is dry, like we're on a date or something. We're not though.

But we are alone.

God.

This man has whipped me and punished me, when I was naked and vulnerable, and I'm worried about getting things just right?

With trembling hands, I place a blueberry muffin on a plate and head over to him. I slide the plate on the table in front of him.

"Your breakfast, sir," I say, intending to make a joke of it, but the words make my cheeks flush and he doesn't laugh.

"Thank you, Chandra. Now go get yourself something to eat." He folds his hands in his lap and doesn't touch the food on the plate, waiting for me to obey.

It's the smallest of things, but it makes my belly warm. I missed this. God, I missed this, having someone care for me and make sure I take care of myself. I do the bare minimum now. I throw myself into my work and go hours, sometimes full days even, without eating. Then I grab whatever's nearby without thought. I get so immersed in things, I don't get enough sleep like I should. If someone asked me, I'd deny the fact that I need a keeper, but being with him again? It feels nice.

I grab a cranberry-orange muffin and make myself a cup of tea, my hands shaking with nerves. I need to steady them. I'm tired, though, I tell myself. It's got to be the fatigue.

But it's more than that.

Joining him, I place my plate down next to his, but before I can sit he's standing and pulling out a chair for me. I give him a bashful smile.

"Thank you."

God, this feels so right.

He sits back down and sips his coffee. "That's some damn good coffee," he says. "I don't remember Marla stocking blueberry muffins. Her specialty is the lemon cake."

"I made the muffins," I tell him.

Folding back the wrapper, he takes a bite and his eyes go wide. "That's delicious," he says around a mouthful of crumbs.

"You always did love my baking."

We fall quiet, eating our breakfast, but I only nibble. I'm too nervous to eat much, and my eyes are so heavy the lids feel like they're weighted. I yawn again, cover my hand with my mouth, then take another sip of tea.

"Why are you so tired?" he asks, leaning back in his chair.

"I didn't sleep much last night," I tell him. "I… well, let's just say I was inspired." I look away bashfully. I can't meet his eyes.

"Good," he says. "Well, good that you were inspired. Inspired to do what?"

"Write."

"Then my evil plan worked."

I smile. "Yup. And, excuse me, but I believe that was *my* evil plan."

"It was your evil wish. I was the plan maker."

I snort. "Okay, fair enough."

Sobering, he asks, "Exactly what time did you get to bed?"

Uh oh.

I fold my muffin wrapper in quarters. "Umm…"

He was always such a stickler for these things. And why do I love that?

"Um isn't a good enough answer." His tone sharpens, folding his arms on his chest. "Tell me."

"Well, I didn't," I finally respond. "Not really. I wrote all night and finally crashed for an hour or so?"

"Chandra," he says, warning in his voice. "I'm thrilled you were inspired, and I'll do my best to make sure I keep you inspired, but you don't neglect your sleep to write."

He'll do his best to keep me inspired?

"Um, we do though," I say. "People do. Like,

writers do. We write all the time and often neglect sleep or something equally beneficial for the sake of the written word."

That just earns me a stern brow raise. "Oh?"

I push on. "Creativity can't be corralled," I say, like I'm in court defending myself. I don't even know if I believe this, but for some reason I need to explain it to him. "So when the muse comes knocking, I have to answer that door." I sound ridiculous.

He tips his head to the side and a corner of his lips twitch. "Muse comes knocking," he repeats.

"Yes. The muse. The... you know... inner voice that tells me it's time to write."

His lips twitch again.

"I know what a muse is. Baby, this *outer* voice is stepping in and telling your inner voice that your ass gets to bed, or your ass gets punished."

Cue the tingle. It's not fair how easily he does that.

I swallow. "Are we scening?"

At that, he sobers. "We're not." Taking my much smaller hands in his larger ones, he holds my gaze with his. "Do I have to be scening with you to tell you what to do? I never did before. We didn't 'scene.' We were just us."

I swallow. I don't know how to answer this.

"You said you were going to become a regular at Verge," he continues.

"Mhm." Feeling him touch me again reignites my insides. I'm aroused and humbled and curious.

"So we'll see what I can do under the circumstances. But until further notice, you're in bed by ten so you get a good night's sleep." He holds one of my wrists against his rough fingers and glides the thumb along my pulse. "Do they hurt after a long day of writing?" He continues massaging until I feel the tension I didn't even know I had ebb away.

"Sometimes," I tell him. "Especially after a particularly long day of writing."

He nods. "And how do you have time to work here and write?"

"I only work here part time."

"I see." He waits, and when I don't speak, he quirks an eyebrow at me.

"What?"

"I asked you a question, Chandra," he says. "I'm waiting for the answer."

Shit! What did he ask again? Something about finding time to work and write. "Oh, so, I write on my breaks and when I go home at night. I'm… sort of a night owl. I write a lot then."

"I see. Tell me what you wrote last night."

Now my cheeks are flaming. It was the hottest ménage scene I've ever written. Clamping my lips together, I give him a look that says *oh hell no*.

Narrowing his eyes, he returns that look with a *oh yes you will*.

We stare in a battle of wills. Part of me wants to tell him.

"Need to find out for myself?" he asks. "Alright, then. What's your pen name?" He lets go of my hands and stands up, heading to the large display of kinky romance books Marla's running a sale on.

"I'm not telling!"

Turning to me, he anchors his hands on his hips. "I need to spank it out of you?"

My heart races. "I shouldn't have to tell you my pen name on threat of a spanking!"

But immediately my mind goes to him bending me over the little table right here and slamming his palm against my ass.

"So," he says, a hard edge taking over his voice. "You let perfect strangers read your books but not me?"

"It isn't like that." I'm circling the books, trying to get him away. If he sees what I write, I'll die. I'm not sure why, but I know it to be true.

"Oh?" he asks.

On instinct, my eyes flit to the huge display of glossy paperbacks I've signed, adorned with a golden sticker on the front that says *Signed by the Author*.

"Bingo."

Damn it. I've watched enough C.S.I. to know that a guilty party's gaze will frequently go straight to the evidence they're trying to hide. The throw rug that covers the hidden key. The closet door that hides the body.

The bookshelf where all my books sit.

I'm my own worst enemy.

I let out a sigh as he lifts a paperback in hand and raises a brow at the cover, all glossy skin and sex appeal. Turning it over in his hand, he reads the blurb.

"Don't," I plead, but he's got that glint in his eye that tells me he's not stopping now.

"When single mother Elena Mcintosh finds herself at her neighbor's mercy, she—"

"Axle," I plead.

Mercifully, he stops, but only so he can open up the cover and read.

"Nooo," I moan.

His mouth drops open and his eyes crinkle around the edges. "With the purposeful intent of a master at work, he glides his tongue over my—"

I'm going to die. No, I'm already dead. I cover my face with my hands, trying to drown out his bark of laughter as he continues reading. He flips pages and doesn't stop for minutes while I die a slow death.

"Baby, this is *good*. It's the real deal. I'm just messin' with you."

I peek out from behind my hands. "Yeah?"

"*Yeah*," he says. "And listen, I haven't read this whole thing, but I know for a fact Marla wouldn't have put these on display like this if she didn't think they were top quality."

My hands drop. "Top quality?"

He nods, his approval filling me up like sunshine, from the top of my head all the way down to my toes.

"Why do you want to know what I write so badly?" I ask him.

He shrugs a shoulder. "We need to get reacquainted. And why do you like to make me coffee and bring me breakfast?"

That makes me grow a little shy. "Well… I like serving you." It's true. There's a part of me that's a natural submissive, who wants to earn his praise and approval.

Reaching out, he tugs a lock of my hair. "You're a good girl, Chandra."

The door to the shop jangles open and we step apart like we're totally guilty.

God.

Marla walks in, blinking wide eyes at us. "Well, hello," she says. "Master Axle. I see you've met my newest hiree?" She walks briskly past us and removes her coat, hat, and gloves, hanging them up on a peg behind the counter.

"I've known Chandra longer than this store's been around," Axle says. Well, so much for keeping anything secret.

"Is that right?" she asks. "How do you know each other?" She shoots me a quizzical look, and I feel a little guilty. I should've maybe told her about last night.

"I… grew up in the neighborhood where he was… well…" My voice trails off and Axle laughs out loud, but the door to the shop opens at that moment and Marla gets busy handling her customer.

"What should I tell her?" I hiss to him.

Axle just wraps a hand around the back of my neck and gives me a firm but tender squeeze. "Babe, let me handle this."

Well I like that. "Sure," I say, as the customer leaves with his purchase and Marla turns back to us.

"Spill, girl," she says. "I've known Axle for

years, and it's blowing my mind that you two know each other."

What's he going to tell her?

"She was a young girl, right out of high school, when we met," he says. "I was a newly-ordained priest who lived on her street. We fell in love, had an illicit affair, then broke it off when things got too intense."

Marla blinks. Her mouth hangs open, mirroring mine. He did *not*.

"Well," I say with a sardonic laugh, "Maybe you should tell her the truth now? Stop hiding the facts?"

"And now," he continues, as if there is nothing at all scandalous or wrong about this, "I found her again. As you're well aware, I'm no longer a priest. She's a full-grown woman. And here we are." My heart's doing strange, wonderful, fluttery things in my chest. Marla's grinning. But soon, it fades, because he's drawing closer to me, his hand on the back of my neck is pulling me to him. Then he's kissing me, right here in the store, just a quick brush of lips.

I close my eyes when he comes back in for more. I can't even care that Marla's here, that anyone could walk in at any minute, that I'm a new person now that he doesn't even know, and how can he make this claim on me?

Because this is right. Perfect.

Necessary.

I need more, which is exactly what he wants from me. I lean into the kiss while Marla whoops out loud. The door to the bookstore clangs again and I'm only mildly troubled, because he's still kissing me and hell, I'm not stopping this.

"Books, and cake, and kisses?" The accent gets my attention, and Axle lets me go. Viktor stands the entryway.

"Honey, it's 'buy a book, get a kiss day,'" Marla says. "What book will you have?"

"Five of whatever *he* bought," Viktor says.

"Limited edition," Axle grits out, and I think he's the only one not amused.

"We're talking about books," I whisper in his ear.

"*You're* talking about books," he amends.

Viktor walks to Axle and extends his hand. "Viktor," he says. "Not sure we've had the pleasure of meeting."

"Axle." They shake so hard it looks painful, and I wince involuntarily. Well then. It looks like I just walked right into a pissing match.

Viktor finally lets go and turns to Marla, and they go back behind the desk and talk to one another. Axle helps me stock some shelves, place sale tags on new releases in the front, and fill some online orders we got overnight.

Axle picks up his order and takes the trash out. When he's gone, Marla turns to me. "Girl, you know Axle's a dom, right? And a damn good one. I've scened with him a few times."

A flourish of jealousy hits my chest, but I tamp it down, and Viktor's jaw tightens.

"I know," I tell her. "I *definitely* know he's a dom."

A smile lights up her face. "Girl, we have some catching up to do."

I grin. "Tonight at Verge?"

She nods. "It's a date."

Viktor frowns at Marla. "Are you planning on going this evening?"

She nods. "Well, yes. I go most evenings."

He stands with arms folded on his chest. "Did I give you permission?"

Marla's eyes widen, and she flushes pink. "Um, no," she stammers, but thankfully Axle walks in at that moment. I'm not sure I like seeing my friend chastised by this guy, and the whole "permission" thing is still new to me.

"Chandra, I need to get going," Axle says. Standing by the door, he beckons for me to come over to him. I gratefully leave Marla to deal with Viktor and walk to Axle.

"Axle," I whisper in his ear. "Is it normal for a guy to demand someone to ask for permission when he's only known her for twenty-four hours?"

Looking over my shoulder, Axle frowns, then he leans in to whisper in my ear. "Babe, it's normal for a *dom* to demand his sub ask permission when he's known her for minutes."

"That's when they're scening," I hiss.

He holds up a hand. "And you know they're not?"

I look back over at them. Viktor's got a grip on Marla's elbow, and her head is down. I wonder if this is my writer's imagination or if this is actually okay. I shrug at Axle.

"Keep an eye on things, but stay out of it,"

Axle says, and there's warning in his voice. "Things get complicated when people interfere in other people's relationships, especially a dom/sub one like this when you definitely don't know the whole picture."

I frown at him, my pride prickling. "You were the one who told me to keep an eye on things," I say, but he gives me a warning look.

"Chandra, enough."

I close my mouth in surprise. He's got that stern look in his eyes, and I didn't expect it. When he has my attention, he raises a finger to me to catch my attention.

"Are you allowed to talk back?"

I don't actually know what I'm allowed to do, so I answer him honestly. "I don't know. I mean obviously you're not a fan."

He shakes his head, but his eyes are twinkling when he tugs a lock of my hair. "Meet me at Verge tonight, and I'll clarify things for you. I'd pick you up, but I have to go a lot earlier and you'll still be here."

My heart beat thunders and my mouth goes dry. We've already talked about this, and still, my mouth goes dry. "Yes, sir," I say. "I'll be there. What time?"

"Seven o'clock, and I want you to bring a change of clothes."

My skin is all prickly with excitement and nerves, my belly is doing crazy flip flops.

"Okay," I whisper, then nod. I grin at him. "I mean *yes, sir*."

The parting kiss he gives me takes my breath

away, slow and languid and dominant, taking what's his and leaving me hoping for more. His fingers tangle in my hair and I anchor my arms on his shoulders. I come up on my toes and lose myself to him, in strength and memories, a part of who I once was resurrecting when I'm in his arms. Too soon, he releases me and tugs a lock of my hair with a lopsided grin.

"Behave," he says.

"What happened to *we don't kiss?*" I ask. What are we doing here?

"That's at the club," he reminds me. "No kissing. No fucking."

My pulse spikes. Then he's gone.

One day ago, I was going about my life, making my way in this world. I was working and making friends and paying bills and buying groceries, washing my laundry and walking along never knowing how quickly that would all change. That a man would walk into my present straight from my past and bring me to my knees, leaving me longing for the man I loved then and love now. There's a hole in my heart when he leaves, as if a part of my very self just walked away.

Tonight, then.

I turn back to the store, not entirely sure what's going on here at all. Marla's looking at me in stunned silence, her eyes wide and mouth slightly parted. Viktor's just left, and she's got the freshly-tousled, just-kissed look about her.

"Well, then," she whispers. "Time for a coffee break?"

Chapter Eleven

Axle

Tobias takes a long pull from a travel mug of coffee and leans back in his chair. Zack's just arrived, and Tobias has locked and shut his door, an indication that something's off, because I've never seen him do that. I stare at both of them, needing answers. Two days ago, this was a club filled with people I cared about, my friends, and I'd have done anything to be sure the members were safe.

Now, my girl's coming here. So I won't rest until I know I can bring here safely.

"Axle." Zack greets me with a chin lift, pulls out a chair, and takes a seat and runs a hair through his longish, sandy-brown hair. Zack's one of the more serious members here, a stickler for rules and safety, and even though we give him shit for being a stick-in-the-mud sometimes, he's a good guy.

"Zack."

Tobias puts his coffee down and leans over his desk, his fingertips pressed together. Tobias is a large man, with his broad shoulders and dark hair and eyes. His face is fuller since he married his wife Diana, and he's got more laugh lines around his eyes than he used to. Marriage becomes him. Zack and Tobias are the two pillars of Club Verge, and over the years have become my closest friends.

This is a sparse but well-furnished office with large, comfortable leather chairs, a gleaming desk outfitted with a computer and office supplies, and monitors set up along the walls that show the vacant rooms of Verge. If I didn't know those clipboards held BDSM contracts, I'd think this looked like any normal office. The cameras are on full display, as all of them monitor the public rooms.

"Axle wanted to talk to me about something he noticed the other night during the blizzard," Tobias says, cutting right to the chase.

Zack, our friend and member here, a detective for the NYPD, is our go-to when anything arises. He raises his eyebrows to me and leans back in his chair.

"I don't have much," I tell him. There's no way of telling him everything without mentioning Chandra. Hell, after kissing her at the bookstore, word's gonna get out soon eventually. And I'm not turning back. So now's as good a time as any.

Leaning back in the chair, I clasp my fingers behind my head. "When I closed the other night,"

I tell them. "I thought we were totally vacant but neglected to check the women's restroom. When I did, I found a young woman who was sick, and she hadn't heard our announcement to evacuate."

Zack nods. I can feel Tobias' eyes on me, steady and certain. He's seen more than anyone else has yet, though I like to believe the more intimate things were for my eyes only.

"She was a girl I knew back in the day," I continue. I take in a breath and let it out on a sigh. These guys are my friends. There's nothing to hide. "I knew her back when I lived another life. When I was a small-town priest."

Zack's eyes widen almost comically, and he sits up straight. "Axle," he says. "Say that one more time?"

I laugh humorlessly, the memory still sad and painful. Tobias knows my past, but only the bare minimum. "I was a priest," I repeat. "Newly ordained. I moved into the rectory on the same street where Chandra lived with her parents."

Neither of them says anything, but I can feel the burning question.

"She was legal," I say through clenched teeth. The thought of taking advantage of a minor makes acid churn in my stomach, but I plod on. They need to know that fact. "She was an adult, but still living with her parents. Came from a strict home, and actually had an arranged marriage set up." I lift my chin, my voice rising in strength as I tell my story. "I loved her from the moment I first met her. She wasn't mine to have, and I wasn't hers, but we did it anyway. We fell in love. We had an affair. And when someone found out about it, they leaked our news to the local press with pictures of us together." I swallow hard. "Condemning pictures." The memory of those pictures plastered over the local paper are seared into my memory for life, a constant chastisement for the mistakes I've made. "We broke it off and went our separate ways."

Zack asks the last thing I expect. "What priest has the name *Axle?* And the tats?" Tobias chuckles.

"My name was Noah," I tell him. "Axle was a nickname I picked up at the shop, and it stuck. No one calls me Noah anymore, and the tats came after I was laicized."

"Laicized?"

It all comes back with ease, all the trappings of the faith I left. Hell, I could recite the words of mass right now.

"It means to become a lay person. No longer a priest."

"Stripped of his super powers," Tobias says with a smirk.

Zack nods. "Got it. And so this girl shows up one night at your BDSM club?" he asks speculatively.

"Yeah," I tell him. "It was an accident. If you knew her, you'd know she isn't the type to play games. And night before last, I found her puking her guts out in the bathroom."

Tobias snorts. "Romantic reunion."

He has no idea. Good.

But Zack looks disbelieving, and his suspicion irritates me.

"Isn't a little odd," he says, "that she just shows up and sees you again? Do you believe she's telling the truth? How do you know she didn't stake you out?"

I can picture her innocent eyes looking at mine, and I know there's no way she planned this. No way she lied.

"She didn't stake me out," I say through clenched teeth.

"Okay," Zack says. "I'm happy for you, man, if you are. But how does this play into why we're here today?"

I nod. "So she was totally fine while on the floor and guests were here, then became violently sick almost instantly. I wondered if someone had slipped something into her drink."

Zack furrows his brow, giving me a look that says he's not sure I've got a valid point, but he's too polite to criticize.

"Listen," I tell him. "She hadn't had anything to eat. And after she got it all out of her system, she was fine. No residual side effects like a virus or anything like that."

"Was she drinking on an empty stomach?" Tobias asks. "If she was, she could've just been vomiting because she was drunk?"

I shake my head. "She wasn't drunk. Believe me. Buzzing, maybe, but this was different."

"Got it," Zack says. "Fair enough. So what else did you see?"

"Well, I went back to the bar and found the surveillance cameras over the bar were covered with fabric, as if someone wanted to temporarily mask the feed."

Now Zack looks stern, his lips set in a thin line. "No wires cut?"

I shake my head. "Nope."

"And Tobias, you've gone over the feed?"

Tobias nods. "Yeah. Nothing amiss. One minute, the feed is coming through as usual, the next, things are wobbly then it's black."

"Interesting. But the only guy who would have access to the surveillance cameras by the bar would be Travis, and we all know how much we can trust him."

We do.

Zack looks to Tobias. "Any new members lately?"

Tobias nods. "Lots," he says.

"Guy named Viktor?" I ask. I feel kinda like a douche for bringing him up, and throwing Marla's new man under the bus, but I don't want to leave any evidence behind and I've learned to listen to my gut.

Tobias nods. "Him, and a few of his cousins," he says. "They all come up squeaky-clean, though. Ties to the Russian military, but nothing more. No records. Not even so much as a parking ticket."

"Got it."

"Okay," Zack says. "Tobias, do I have permission to investigate further?"

Tobias nods. "Listen, man, our members' safety is important. You're on my payroll, and they submitted applications, so have at it." He turns back to me. "Literally all we have for information is that Chandra was throwing up, and someone blocked the bar feed?"

I nod, suddenly feeling foolish. I wish I had more, and it was enough that I didn't want to neglect mentioning it, but hell I'm not about to let this slide. My girl's safety is on the line, and if anyone threatened that…

Tobias nods, too. "Well, now we know, so let's keep an eye on things?"

"Absolutely."

"I'll give Travis a call and check in with him," Zack says.

"Right," Tobias says. "Check back in tomorrow, everyone's on alert tonight. I'll fill in Braxton and Chloe, too. Definitely helps having a private investigator and cop on the lookout."

"Good call," I say, getting to my feet.

"Chandra coming here tonight?" Tobias asks.

I nod. "Yeah."

He smiles at me. "Good."

I leave the office unsettled. I don't want to talk to them about Chandra and whatever is going on with us now. Hell, she's coming here tonight. They'll see her soon enough. And I'm not even sure what I'll tell them even if I did talk about her. When I get to my private room, I don't know if it's my imagination or that I just want her here, because I imagine her still in my bed, the room illuminated with her light and permeated with her lingering, intoxicating scent. My cock throbs at the memory of her naked and stripped, and hell I want her back here.

Next, I check the linens to be sure I'm well

stocked. Towels and washcloths, blankets and clean sheets line the small utility closet in the bathroom. The plastic grocery bag I brought with me contains a whole variety of feminine things I imagine she needs. I went to the "travel size" section of the store and bought anything that looked pink and lavender and feminine. I wasn't even really sure what I was buying. I should maybe up my girly toiletry game. I'll have to pay closer attention.

Next, I make sure the small, dorm-sized fridge I have here has water and fresh fruit, a few sandwiches, and a variety of snacks.

Then, the toy table.

Anticipation curls in my belly when I make my way to the implements. I'll outfit this section. Soon. But not tonight. For some reason, the idea of wielding anything on her doesn't appeal to me like it has in the past, and it's a little disconcerting. I've always loved gripping the handle of a paddle or crop or my sturdy leather belt. But when I think about it, I make up my mind. With Chandra, I want nothing between us but the intimacy of skin to skin contact.

The cleaners have been in, and the bed is freshly made, the floors mopped, the bathroom immaculate. I smile to myself. Now all I need is her.

Am I getting my hopes up too soon, though? I've convinced myself she's the girl I've always known, but I don't know that to be true. Is she the same girl I met and fell in love with all those years ago, or does she carry with her the scars of her past that will hold her back from me?

And does it matter?

I'm not the same man she knew back then. I've learned better self-control. I know more about who I am, what I need, and what I have to offer others.

I don't wear the collar anymore. And I no longer pretend to be pious.

My job is to prove to her that my devotion hasn't waned, that I've grown into maturity, and without the trappings of the vows I made, I'm a man she can trust. I'll take care of her, protect her, and give her what she needs. Learn what her secrets are and cherish them. Learn what her fears are and slay them. Fill in the holes between when we split up and where we are now until I've mended the torn parts of our relationship and sewn us back together. I'll make it my mission to get to know every bit of her so that I can do what I've always been meant to do.

Love her.

I leave my private room and head to the dungeon. Members have begun to trickle in, now that the sun has set, people are leaving their jobs, dinnertime is over. A few sit by the bar and I scan them over, but everyone's familiar. Nothing unusual.

Chandra's due any minute.

Now, it's time to play.

As I walk to the bar I ask myself, who was the guilty party? It couldn't have been accidental. Someone covered the camera for a reason, and I want to know what those reasons were. I glance at the clock on the wall. She's supposed to be here at seven. She has eight minutes.

I check the snacks we have at the bar, refill the napkin dispenser, and when Travis shows up, we chat about what happened. We're discreet, though, and don't want to be overheard, so he just nods and says, "I'm on it."

I believe him. He's got the natural protective instincts of a dominant every bit as much as I do.

Travis pulls me a beer, and I sit at the bar stool sipping it. Finally, the time has passed. She's due in one minute. I'll wait in the lobby for when she arrives. I push my empty beer stein to Travis and head to the lobby, my palms sweaty and stomach in knots like I'm a freshman about to go on his first date, and nearly crash into Braxton in the doorway. Chloe's standing next to him, her dark hair pulled back, dressed in a short, tight black play dress.

"Watch where you're going," Braxton says, playfully punching my arm. "*Father.*"

I growl at him. "Don't. Don't go there, Braxton."

I push past, so I can get to the lobby. But he's our resident wiseass, and he doesn't shut up.

"Forgive me, father, for I have sinned," he says, with mock repentance. "I gave my girl a righteous spanking for mouthing off to me, which led to much bigger and better things, but she was late for work and I made her call in sick. I made her lie, father." Chloe stands behind him, snickering.

I want to deck the smug grin right off his face.

He's a good friend, and I know he's just joking, but this isn't something I want to kid about.

"Shut it, Brax."

Bowing his head and folding his hands in a prayerful position, he murmurs, "Just give me my penance and I will leave you, father."

The knuckles on my hand tingle, and I make a fist. I won't rise to the bait, though. Instead, I refuse to even smirk and choose to ignore him. Chloe stands in the doorway, trying not to laugh, but I quickly forget my own anger when Chandra walks in the room.

She's holding a little bag that hopefully holds a change of clothes, but the bag is larger than her entire skimpy little outfit. The cherry red top looks like it was tattooed on her, dipping low in the front and revealing full, gorgeous cleavage. The hem comes above her navel, revealing a perfect torso with a gleaming gem of a belly button ring at the center. How'd I miss that before? Maybe she didn't have it in. I want to run my tongue down her belly and make her shiver, then punish her for marring her perfect skin.

Flimsy, glittery black material covers her hips in what's—I don't know, a skirt? Pair of shorts? They're so tight and short I can't tell.

"Hi," she says a little shyly.

"Hi," I respond. "What the hell are you wearing?"

Her face falls and I feel like a douchebag, but only for a minute. Another guy walks into the lobby, tall and blonde, and stares at her. "You got a dom for tonight?" he asks.

Is he serious?

"Yeah, she's got a dom for tonight," I tell him, my voice holding an edge of warning. For Christ's sake. "And the night after that, and the night after *that*."

Braxton chuckles behind me, then I hear him leave.

I don't know what I'm telling myself, or what I'm even declaring to him. To anyone, for that matter. The man holds up a palm as if to tell me he's laying off, then walks through the door to the bar. Chandra blinks at me, then to my surprise, her eyes darken.

"What the hell was that?"

"Excuse me?"

"You just declared ownership of me."

"This surprises you?" I cross my arms on my chest, surprised by the affronted look she's giving me.

"We haven't discussed this yet."

I take her hand and pull her none too gently into the bar area. "I think it's time we had that talk. Don't you?"

"I—well…" she stammers.

"Good. That's what I thought."

"Axle," she says as we move quickly. "You seem angry. Why do you seem so angry?"

"I'm not angry," I tell her. "I'm determined. But you have your safeword," I remind her.

That makes her freeze.

"Chandra." My tone holds warning.

"Yes," she says. "Yes, sir, I have my safeword. Geez, you don't believe in foreplay, do you?"

God. So damn cute.

"Never said that," I tell her. "Give me time, and I'll show you. Did you forget how long I made you wait the other night?"

We enter the bar, now much fuller than earlier, and I take a minute to glance around again. Zack stands sentry over by the pool tables, and Tobias and Diana are in the hall as if they've just emerged from the dungeon or a private room. Brax and Chloe are on their way to the dungeon now. We've got this place tricked out with capable people. I can take some time with Chandra.

She wants foreplay? I'll give her foreplay.

I pat a stool next to me, and she shops on up, but as she does, her skirt rides up so high I can see the lower curve of her ass.

Leaning in, I run my fingers along the back of her neck and tell her, "I should redden that ass of yours for wearing something so skimpy." She leans into me, her pretty voice smooth as silk.

"Maybe you should. Does that mean when you find out I'm not wearing panties I'm getting punished?"

Jesus. My cock lengthens, and I draw closer to her.

"You are in so. Much. Trouble."

"Get you two a drink?" Travis asks, wiping his hands on a bar mop.

I order both of us a drink, taking her hand in mine as I scan the bar again.

"Why are you on edge tonight?" Her hand comes to rest on my knee. "You're acting like everyone's packing a weapon and you're ready to throw down."

Travis pushes the icy glasses over to us, shoots me a grin, then walks away. I hand her her drink and take a sip of mine.

"Just watching things," I tell her. "It's just how I am."

"It's how you always were," she says quietly. Silently, I wrap both of my hands around one of hers. I let her go once. I won't make that mistake again.

"Axle? God, it's weird calling you that, but I guess it makes things a little easier. Like this time, it isn't Father Noah I'm with but a different man. And I don't have that guilt tugging at my conscience like I used to."

She felt guilty before? I let myself believe it was somehow freeing for her to be with me, but of course it wasn't. It was risky as hell, and she knew the consequences if we were found out would threaten her future.

"And yet you *are* still the same person," she says. "That's what I love."

"Should I call *you* something different?" I love teasing her.

Turning her whole body to face me, her eyelids lower and she looks at me from beneath the crescent of full, black lashes. "I thought you already did." I watch as she swallows, and she tugs her lower lip between her teeth before leaning closer to me and dropping her voice to a whisper. "Baby. Little girl…" her voice trails off and she won't meet my eyes. "Maybe over time we can move to the better terms."

"Better?"

She shrugs. "Slave. Babygirl. Little one."

Someone's done her homework. Tugging a lock of her hair, I ask her, "What's it gonna be? Slave or babygirl?"

That gets her gaze back on mine, her round, dark eyes eager. "Not slave, sir."

No. Submissive fits her, but not at the level of total self-denial. As much as she likes the sterner side of things, she's always craved the tender affection, too. I cup my hand around her jaw and kiss her forehead.

I was a total dumbass for ever thinking "hands off" was the right choice. Hell no. This is Chandra.

"Screw no kissing," I rumble, leaning in closer so that her breath stirs against my cheek when I whisper in her ear. "Be my babygirl?"

I can almost feel her visibly melt like butter. "Yes. Yes, please."

I lean in and kiss her.

Chapter Twelve

Chandra

He keeps me so close to his side I'm almost glued to him, and if anyone had a doubt before now that I was his, that doubt's vanished. He may as well tattoo it straight across my forehead and toss a collar around my neck. But the protective, possessive vibe he's thrown around us is clear enough I don't need a collar or any of the other outward signs that he owns me.

My first instinct was to fight it, but I love how possessive and jealous he is.

I want more than this, though, and I'm not sure yet what. A part of me has lain dormant, like a bud buried beneath the surface of the ground, and I've only just begun to feel the rays of sun that let me live. I want to stretch myself heavenward and soak that up, flourish as I was meant to, no longer held apart from what makes me whole.

He makes me whole.

I see now that when I was apart from him, I grew into who I was meant to be. He grew into who he was meant to me. We're not strangers who just met each other. We haven't changed. We've *evolved*. Grown.

And now… now that I'm with him again, I don't ever want to let him go.

I want to sit by his feet and rest my head on his knees while he runs his hands through my hair and reads, or watches TV. I want to kneel by him and serve him, and feel his praise bask over me like sunlight breaking through clouds, warm and bright and nourishing. I want to get over myself, let him read my books that hold the words I draw from my soul and weave onto paper, a visible sign of who I am and what I've accomplished. I want to cook him dinner and wash his clothes and do all the domestic things my friends scorn because it would be for *him*.

Hell, I want to have his babies.

"Do you remember how we used to walk in the cemetery?" he asks. He's led me to the dungeon and brought me over to a quiet corner of the room. A small but sturdy loveseat waits for us, covered in crimson fabric. Folding himself onto one side, he reaches for my waist and draws me onto his lap. My much smaller frame melts into his and I lean against his chest, resting my head on his shoulder. His grip tightens around me, and my heart flutters rapidly in my chest.

"Of course," I tell him.

His grip tightens in warning, and I remember where we are.

"Sir," I amend. "Of course, sir. Silly as it sounds, I always felt I was safe with you in the cemetery because you were a priest and you could ward off any demons that endangered me."

He snorts. "Ward off demons? I had too many of my own."

"Had?" I ask him, not teasing at all now. "Do you still have any?" I admire a man who can own his own flaws and still fight them, still get up every day and face whatever it is he needs to.

"Do we ever lose the demons?" he asks. "It's a constant battle, you know. Good and evil. Right and wrong. Selfish or selfless."

I don't respond at first, but instead take a moment to observe what's happening around us. It's different than it was before, now that I'm on his lap being held by him, as if the intensity of the scenes are muffled, like a buffer of sorts. To my right, a woman has a collared man at her feet. She's lecturing him and holding him in place with the crimson red leather tongue of a crop against his ass. He nods, and she gives him a little smack of approval. Someone at the cross is about to get a whipping, the spanking benches are occupied, and the other loveseat hosts a threesome, a woman kneeling before two strong, sturdy men, bare chested, clad only in leather pants.

And I wonder. Right here, while the club members pursue their interests, isn't this the battle of selfish versus selfless? Good and evil? Right and wrong? They need to trust one another, and they strip away all that holds them back when they bring their bared, vulnerable selves here to play, both dom and sub alike. When given the choice, submissives can choose to retain their own control or relinquish it to someone else. Dominants wield authority that has the power to build or destroy.

The trappings of dynamics and power play don't diminish the very real struggles, heartaches, hopes and dreams, losses and gains, of people who seek to love and be loved.

"You know, you're right," I say to him. "It is a constant battle."

My gaze wanders to his strong, large hands, calloused from work and roughened with labor, the hands that hold me now. I remember those hands on my body, and my pulse races. The sounds of pleasure and pain around us fades until there's only me. Him. Us.

"Did you write today?" he asks.

The question surprises me, and I don't respond right away. I blink. "Oh. Well, yes," I say. "But only a little. I wrote on my lunch break."

"And you normally write at night?"

I nod.

"Because that's when your muse is all happy?"

I grin. "Yeah." It's cute hearing him talk about my muse.

"So how 'bout this," he says in a low, deep drawl, like he's mulling this over. "You bring your computer here. You meet me at the club. I give you something to write about, and when the night's over, you can set up in the private room and tap away at that keyboard."

He wants me to bring my work here?

One boyfriend laughed and told me there was no reason for me to put so much effort into something that wasn't "literary," and that it was important to not let "hobbies take over your life."

Yeah, I dumped his ass.

Another hated the idea of being in any of my books, but the joke was on him. He sucked in bed and didn't have a dominant bone in his body, so he made it into my books alright, but only as the loser ex-boyfriend.

"You'd do that for me?" I ask. I want to hug him and kiss him and change the name of the hero in my current book to his. Until Marla, no one ever took my writing seriously.

"Of course," he says, nodding his head. "Honestly, babe, scening with you is hardly a hardship."

"Glad you'll take one for the team."

He gives me a playful smack on the ass and pulls me close to his chest for a brief kiss to the forehead before he frees me.

"Up you go," he says, sliding my legs off him onto the floor. "I want you all to myself, babygirl. I don't want to share. I'm afraid if another dom here touches you, I'd have to break his fingers."

"I see."

"So if you're with me, you're *with me.* You obey my instructions and do what you're told. There is no 'on and off' with me at the club. We can come here to play or to meet friends, but I want all of your submission. And I promise that I'll cherish that. You won't regret it."

I write about women who are strong and

curious about the lifestyle, and some who crave this lifestyle because submission is so intrinsically woven into who they are, their very identity involves choosing submission. I know and have known for years—since *my Noah*—that I'm the one who craves all of it. I'm not satisfied with play, and I don't need to battle for power or control. I crave the constant protection, attention, and focus of the man who loves me and literally no man I've ever met has fed that need in me.

I've been starving for true dominance. I tasted it once and he ruined me on men forever.

"Yes, sir," I tell him, earnest and eager. "Let's try it. Right now?"

He sobers, his voice dropping to deep and stern. "Yes. Right now. Because it's time I punish you for wearing that outfit."

Every threat of punishment makes me tingle, part fear, part arousal, and I don't understand it, but I don't really need to. I don't respond, because my mouth is dry, and I don't know what to say. While I walk beside him, tucked so close to him we're practically attached at the hip, I notice how others part, giving him a wide berth, watching him with a measure of respect and deference. My heart swells. That's *my* man they admire and respect.

"Master Axle," some greet as we walk. He nods and greets them but gives no one his undivided attention. No one but me. He whispers in my ear and points a few things out, weaves his fingers through mine and holds me close. We walk together like he's leading me in a dance and I'm taking his lead, easily falling into step. We head out of the dungeon and down the hall toward his room.

I'm not sure what I need or where he's leading me, but I know I'm going to follow.

"Did you eat dinner?" he asks.

"Yup."

"Good girl. You tired?"

"Not yet, sir." I pause and stifle a yawn. Adrenaline's fueling me now, but I don't want to lie to him. "Well, maybe a little, yeah."

The door to his room swings open and he welcomes me inside first. My heart races when the sound of the door clicks shut, but I don't have any time to think about that, because as soon as the door shuts, I'm pinned up against it, and he yanks one knee up and wraps it around him. The touch of his hand at my throat makes me shiver, I can breathe but barely. I take in a shuddering breath while his eyes bore into me.

"Mine," he says, before leaning in to kiss me. I squeeze my knee against his hip, my pussy flush up against him, and when he brushes his lips against mine, he swallows my moan. I'm melting, liquid flesh and bones undone when I'm around him. A throb of arousal thrums between my legs, and I grind my hips against him. My skin prickles with warmth and heat, my pulse racing with excitement and anticipation. Flames flicker along my skin when he releases my mouth and takes my lip between his teeth, biting, claiming. Fingertips dig into my ass, so hard I know he's claiming ownership.

I need this. I crave this. If he doesn't make love to me, I'll lose my fucking mind.

"You'll dress appropriately," he tells me in my ear.

"How—ohhh," I moan as he slides his tongue along my collarbone and grazes it with his teeth. "How does one dress appropriately here?"

"I'll buy you clothes," he says, before he takes my ear lobe between his teeth.

"I have clothes," I moan.

"Not anymore," he responds. I shiver when his fingers tickle between my thighs, so close but not close enough. Rocking my pelvis does no good, as he slaps my ass good and hard for trying to make him touch me.

"Babygirl," he growls. "When I punish you, I want you bared. Strip."

I like that. *Babygirl.* Yeah, I like that a lot.

Letting me go, he crosses his arms and stands, feet planted, waiting for me to obey. This I can get into.

When I knew him before, our moments together were often stolen and hurried. Hushed conversations. Whispered promises. Intimate moments in the back of his car, behind locked doors, hidden and desperate.

Now, we have nowhere else to go, nothing else to do, but revel in each other.

I stand in front of him in the tiny skirt and top that I really *did* think was appropriate for here, holding his gaze with mine. The light hits the silver at his temples, and it makes my heart throb. His eyes, blue flecked with gray, so stern and piercing, look at me with a tenderness that makes a lump rise in my throat. I want to look away, but I couldn't if I tried, held in that gaze. But when I slide the zipper down my hip, his eyes move downward, and I watch his Adam's apple bob up and down as he swallows, the only indication he's fighting for self-control. The fabric's so tight, I have to forcibly push my skirt down, baring my naked ass and full hips.

If I ever doubted he was attracted to my figure, there is absolutely zero doubt in my mind now. The air in the room's so electric, my own breath comes in short, ragged gasps, and my fingers shake when I reach for the hem of my top. I close my eyes and inhale. It's got a built-in shelf bra, so once that's off, I'm bare to him and I'm definitely not used to that yet.

I take my time, lifting the top so slowly my hands shake, wanting to tease him with slow, deliberate moves, but I can't control this now if I tried.

"Jesus," he whispers, a prayer and plea, "you're a fucking goddess."

I shake my head. God, I'm not. I eat too many French fries and I love chocolate chip cookies and I don't work out enough. My boobs are nice enough but the rest of me's just a *tad* too jiggly.

"Don't you dare," he rasps. "You contradict a damn word about how gorgeous you are, and your ass feels my belt."

I close my eyes and let myself relish the heat of his threat. I squeal when I feel him right next to me, his hands on my shirt impatient and eager. I'm divested of my clothing in record time and lifted straight up off the floor. He tosses me, naked and squealing, over his shoulder, and marches to the bed, sitting heavily before he pulls me down and topples me right over his knee.

"You were taking too long," he says. "I lost my patience."

"You never were a patient man," I respond. "Ow!" While I'm still flailing over his knee, his hand crashes down on the fullest part of my ass. I squirm and try to protect myself but with the ease of a master craftsman, he grabs my wrist and pins it to my lower back.

"Oh, no, you don't," he says, and now he's spanking me in earnest. This time, he's only using his palm. God, it's better than the day before, and my heart sings. *This.* His hand against my naked skin hurts so good. I moan, and squirm. I love that when I fight him he doesn't cave but just calmly restrains me and carries on. I could safeword. But hell, why would I?

"I'll dress you in fucking burkas if I need to," he says, spanking me over and over again. "You ever wear something like that again, I'll punish you right where you stand, in front of everyone, then I'll take you back privately and spank you all over again." My ass is flaming hot, and on the surface, I want this to stop, but somehow, deep down inside, I know I'm not ready for him to stop.

"Okay," I tell him. "Yes, sir, I promise. Burkas. Skirts. Capes. Hoods. All the coverage. I promise."

He laughs and spanks me again, and again, then runs his hand along my stinging ass, rough skin gliding over my bruised flesh.

"Whatever you say, sir," I manage to say, but my thighs are wet, my lady parts throb, and there's an emptiness inside me only he can fill. He massages out the sting, a tenderness only the man who inflicted this pain could deliver. My breasts swell and my belly dips, a tightness of desperate need making me whimper. Maybe he mistakes that whimper for pain, because the next minute I'm swept up in his arms and tucked against his chest.

"You'll behave yourself," he whispers. "Won't you, babygirl?"

"Yes," I nod, so wrapped up in longing and need my voice is a choked whisper.

"Good girl," he rasps. "Chandra. Baby. I need you."

"The feeling's mutual," I groan. He's grinning and growling, and something's caught in my throat as a tremor travels through me. He lays me on the bed and spreads me out, positioning my arms above my head and spreading my legs, with a firm tenderness that makes me melt. He wants to fuck me, and hard, but this reunion is deserving of more than a hard fuck. This is a resurrection that was meant to be. A joining of heart and soul in a way that words can't capture.

When his mouth meets mine, I sigh and melt in boneless surrender, wrapping my arms around him so I can anchor myself to him. I close my eyes and welcome the inky darkness, the intimacy of his lips and tongue meeting mine, shooting spikes of electricity through my limbs and between my legs.

He quotes, "You should be kissed and often by someone who knows how."

The reference to one of my favorite love stories of all times is perfect. He's perfect. The Rhett to my Scarlet, but our love story ends together.

My mind conjures up the lines that speak truth, that feed my soul, but I'm too choked up to say them. I feel them, though.

There is no other pearl to be found in the dark folds of life.

This.

This.

Us.

When he moves his lips to my collarbone and kisses me there, my eyes fly open. I want to see him ravish my body. His broad shoulders shadow me, all muscles and strength and power, his hands raking over my body like he's a blind man, like he needs to memorize every hollow and curve of my body. Grinding between my legs, he nudges them further apart.

"I want you in me," I plead. He groans in my ear. If I could crawl into his skin and meld with him I would, and this is the next best thing. I don't want anything between us. I whisper a hurried promise that I'm on birth control, and it's all he needs.

"Easy, baby," he says. "We have all night. And the night after that, and the night after that."

I close my eyes because my heart is full, and he hasn't even made love to me yet. I'm filled to bursting and we've only just begun.

"We do this together," he says, nudging at my entrance.

I nod. "Together."

He slides into me with a groan, and my heart rate spikes. I'm lost to this, to us, riding waves of pleasure as he thrusts with an almost savage claiming. We don't need words, our sweat-slicked bodies melding as one in surrender and forgiveness and unity. I love him. God, I love him, more than I should, more than is healthy, but emotion overrides intellect and I'm lost to him.

"I love you," I whisper in a tortured, garbled jumble of words and longing.

"I love you," he whispers back with another firm thrust. He rocks his hips and I arch into him, needing harder, more, longer. Time fades and my vision blurs as we speak the universal language of love and surrender. He's holding on, watching me, and when my head falls back, and my climax claims me, he lets himself go. We climax together, and I don't know which of us is groaning and which of us is panting. We're all tangled limbs and shattered breaths and pounding hearts.

Rolling over onto his side, still in me, still throbbing and hot and united, he pulls me onto his chest.

"I love you. All of you. Who you were, who you are, and who you're meant to be."

"And I love you," I tell him. There are things I need to tell him, and now's the moment, when we're bared like this.

"I... need to tell you something," I say. Though he's silent, his arms tighten, and he tenses. But I'm safe, and there's nothing I can say he can't handle. If I don't tell him now, I'll lose my nerve.

"There was a baby." I don't expect the sudden tears to spring to my eyes like this. I thought my emotions were already wrung out, but I was wrong. I can't speak beyond that first sentence. My throat closes, a lump so big I can't go on.

"A baby, Chandra?"

With monumental effort, I steady my voice and tell him. I have to. "After we broke up. I found out I was pregnant." He tightens beneath me, but he doesn't respond. He just holds me. "I didn't test, because we were going through so much. You with the church and me with my family and both of us with our hometown. I knew it in my heart but didn't want to confirm it. I finally took the test, and before I could come up with a plan to tell you —and I promise you, I was going to tell you—I…" I'm crying now and he's silent, absorbing my pain and making it easier to bear.

He holds me impossibly tighter, his voice pained. "Baby. Oh, Chandra."

"I lost it," I say, sniffling on his chest, my nose all runny. It feels good, though, to finally tell him, so I don't stop. "It was painful and sudden and one of the hardest things I've ever been through."

"I could have helped you."

I don't respond, because I don't know what to say. I don't know how to make this better. I'm not even sure I have to.

Minutes pass in silence. He needs to process this.

"It was too soon to know if it was a boy or a girl. After the pain passed, I was glad. I know you, and I knew then that if we'd had a baby you'd have felt obligated to raise that child with me. But you couldn't do that then. I couldn't, either. And then I felt guilty that I was glad I didn't carry that baby to term. Like it was my fault."

"No, honey. Don't think that way. There's nothing to feel guilty about. There was no easy answer to that. God, I'm sorry, Chandra. I'm so sorry."

"Me, too. The thought of losing my only tie to you? I wanted to die. For days and weeks, I prayed that I would die. I mourned losing you. *Us.* But I let you go because it was best for us."

He kisses my forehead tenderly and fiercely. "Baby, I felt the same. But that's in the past now, Chandra. The judgment. The mistakes. The baby we lost. Now you're mine, and I'm not ever letting you go."

Chapter Thirteen

Axle

I sit on the padded bench at the little shop I've taken her to. I have no idea where to buy women's clothes, but I asked around at the club, and Beatrice and Diana and Marla all told me this was the place to go to find affordable, beautiful clothes, so here we are.

Ever since that night at the club when she told me everything, I can't let her out of my sight. I hate the thought that she bore that pain without me, the pain we should have borne together, and I'm determined to never let her experience anything like that alone again. *Ever.*

Our jobs keep us busy and I've let her get away with wearing a few of the outfits she already owned. It's almost a game, and one I fucking love to play. She texts me her outfit of the day and I approve or disapprove. It's a pretty simple benchmark: if she's showing cleavage or too many curves, that outfit goes in the donate pile. One morning she got a wild hair and texted me a picture of her wearing a too-short, skimpy silver dress that showed so much cleavage it looked like little more than a negligee. I knew she was probably intentionally being a brat, but I took her straight across my knee for even owning something like that.

She loves it, though. I keep her on a tight leash. She has rules and I keep her accountable. I give her as much freedom as she needs but the control she craves. And I love watching her thrive under my dominance. She gets to bed on time, and no longer subsists on Diet Coke and peanut butter crackers. She tells me her word count on her books has skyrocketed, and I'm the one responsible.

It isn't true, though. It isn't me. It isn't her. It's us.

And now we're here, picking out what will be her wardrobe, approved by me.

"This is a bit high on the controlling spectrum," she says to me, but the way her eyes light up and her cheeks pinken with excitement, I know she loves it.

"Your point?" I get up from the bench and head with her into the shopping plaza to the stores the girls told me about.

"Some people would say you were a control freak," she says, but now she's giggling.

"Still not getting your point," I tell her.

"Maybe you shouldn't tell me what to do," she

says, sticking her tongue out at me. Shopping mall be damned, I give her a good swat to the rear and point to the shop.

"And maybe you don't want to end up tipped over my knee in a shopping mall."

I watch her mouth fall open adorably, and my cock throbs. God, what I wouldn't give to redden her ass right here and now, just to show I could.

"You wouldn't," she whispers, but I can feel her arousal from here. I can practically smell it on her.

Leaning in, I wrap my fingers around the back of her neck and give her a gentle but firm squeeze. "Try me, little girl. Go ahead. Want to see how far you can push me?"

She bites her lip. "Actually, I think I'm good."

"Good girl," I approve. "Let's get you some clothes."

It takes more patience than I have, but I push myself to get through this. I don't know how women can stand this. She's picky, but I'm pickier, and I like pushing her limits. She comes out in a gorgeous purple dress the girls call "eggplant" which makes me roll my eyes. Why can't they just say purple? But this dress makes her skin glow and her eyes look brighter. I love it, but I need to test her.

"Mmm," I say to the saleslady standing by the door. "It's beautiful, but let's see it in red."

"This is *way* too expensive," she argues.

I shake my head at her warningly. "Let me be the judge of that. Now go try on the red."

Chandra's lips thin and she clenches her jaw,

like she's trying to hold herself from snapping at me. She doesn't really want to, though. The saleslady is looking at me like I'm a throwback from some sexist TV show, but I don't give a shit.

"Go," I tell her, flicking a finger toward the dressing room. When she's in there, I hear someone say something I haven't heard in years.

"Father Noah?"

God, no. My stomach clenches before I even see her, and when I look at Veronica Vanderkilt I want to snatch Chandra up and leave this place.

I keep my cool with a curt nod. "Veronica. I'm not Father anymore."

Veronica's a tall, thin, filthy rich woman who made my life and Chandra's a living hell when our scandal hit. She ruled the community with her wealth and power, and when our relationship came to light, she let it be known loud and clear that I needed to be driven out of the church. She stopped at nothing. News reporters. Interviews. Petitions to have my name sullied until the day I died. It's a cruel twist of fate she's here now. For some reason, she doesn't look surprised at all to see me.

Her lips curl. "Oh, that's right. They laicized you, didn't they?"

"They did," I tell her through clenched teeth. "Though it was my own choice."

"Was it?" She tips her head to the side, shooting venom from that gaze. "You had many choices, did you?"

Ignoring her, I take out my phone and shoot Chandra a text.

Stay in that changing room until I tell you. But the phone buzzes in my pocket and I swear to myself. Fuck. I forgot I was holding her phone for her while she changed.

I get to my feet. "I hope you're doing well, Veronica," I lie, stepping toward the changing room.

The saleslady widens her eyes and shakes her head. "You can't come in here, sir. This is women only."

"You work on commission…" my voice trails as I look at her name tag, "Daphne?"

She blinks. "Yes, sir, but that doesn't mean—"

"I'm buying every damn pair of shoes and outfit she's tried on in the 'keep' pile, opening her up an account here, and outfitting her with a few pieces of jewelry and that monthly subscription thing you keep bringing up."

Daphne's eyes widen. "Oh. My."

"Axle?" Chandra steps out of the dressing room, and I swear to God she's a vision. My mouth goes dry when I look at her in the red dress, and I make up my mind. I slam the door and slide the lock in place.

"Sir?" she whispers, a pink flush coloring her cheeks.

"Panties off," I rasp. I need to claim her, right here, right now.

"Axle," she groans when I tug down her panties. Outside the door, Daphne practically runs away, and Veronica's right fucking there, but I don't give a shit. Chandra's mine.

"People will hear," she whispers. I pick up a

silky red and black scarf in her "keep" pile, tie it around her head and order, "bite down on this. Try not to scream."

Her eyes are wide but her pussy's dripping wet. I glide my finger in and out until she coats my hand. I unfasten my belt and unzip my jeans. My cock springs free. She gasps, knowing exactly what I'm about to do and even though her eyes are wide, she grins against the gag.

"I fucking love you," I whisper, before I lift her hips, position my cock at her entrance, and shove her down, impaling her. She drops her head back and moans against the gag but can't say anything. "I loved you then," I say with a savage thrust. "And I love you now. I'll love you until the day I die."

We're panting and desperate, her hands wrapped around the back of my neck while I plunge us fast and furious toward blissful release. She comes around my cock when I lash into her tight, hot cunt. "So perfect." I kiss the side of her cheek.

She giggles as I pull out and pull her panties up. I open the door to the dressing room. Daphne's standing a good distance away, flushed red and clasping at a slim gold necklace at her throat.

"We'll take this dress," I say. "In fact, she's not changing out of it." I tear off the price tag and hand it to Daphne, who watches the whole thing go down with her mouth wide open.

Chandra looks at me in silence but to her credit she doesn't contradict me. She just slides into her shoes and folds up the clothes she wore in here. I take them from her hand and lean into her. "There's a woman from the church out there giving me shit. Don't worry about it. Don't talk to her. Let me handle it."

"Oh, Axle," she whispers. "Really?"

I bend down and brush my lips against hers. "Yeah, baby. But it's okay. Just trust me, okay?"

A soft smile lights her face, and she nods. Daphne rushes in and helps us gather our things, ushering us back into the main area. Veronica's waiting like a predator in the shadows.

"Ah, there she is. My, my," she says, venom dripping from her lips. "The little hussy you ruined your life over."

Ruined my life?

Hell, I just started living.

I laugh so loudly and suddenly Veronica literally jumps and blinks at me in surprise. I turn to my new best friend, Daphne.

"Hey, Daphne? This woman is harassing me. Can you do something about that?"

"Yes, sir," she says, shooting Veronica a glare. "Ma'am, we don't allow customers to harass one another. Please leave, now, before I'm forced to call security."

Veronica blusters and fumes, and actually refuses to leave. While I pay for our purchases, a security officer in a navy-blue uniform escorts her out. Back outside, Chandra is quiet.

"You ok?" I ask her. I thread my fingers through hers and we walk toward the exit.

"I can't believe she would attack you like that after all this time," she says.

"I don't care," I tell her. "We've got nothing to hide now. You're with me, and we're going to do this together. Understand?"

She smiles. "And I can't believe you *did* that."

I lean in to kiss her cheek and whisper, "I'll take you wherever and whenever I want to. God, you're stunning in that dress. Wear it tonight?"

She grins. "Absolutely."

We fall into an easy rhythm of days and nights by each other's sides. She has to work, and so do I, and since the club is easy to access and near both of our jobs, we're here more nights than not, but I never go to bed without her by my side. I work at the auto body shop and she works at Marla's. I visit her on my days off, and she texts me on her lunch breaks. I send her flowers at the bookstore so often that customers begin to joke the new name is "Books and Cups and Flowers."

Even though she's with me at Verge, I don't scene with her in front of anyone else. I'm her dom, and she's my sub, so she gets a good reminder to behave once in a while. She'll sit on my lap and hold my hand when I'm DM for the night. But I don't touch any other women, and no one is allowed to come anywhere near her.

I don't like anything between us. *Anything.* When I play with her, we don't use toys anymore, not since that one day of role play. We don't role play anymore, either. There are no more clamps, plugs, or implements. She wants only my hands, my fingers, my mouth, my tongue. Sometimes the tools of the trade heighten the experience. With Chandra, this is what we need.

She brings her laptop with her as I instructed, and often sits on my lap after we've spent some time with each other, and she writes her little fingers off. She's gotten over her aversion to me reading her books and now asks for my input. Occasionally, I'll read over a scene and give her some ideas or talk over a plot point she needs to wrestle through. She says her words have never flown like this before. I make sure she gets to bed on time and eats good, nourishing food. I spoil her in all ways but one: she's never allowed to be disrespectful or disobedient.

When we arrive at Verge, we go to the bar, but she doesn't have a drink this time. She nibbles on the nuts in the little bowls and sips a soda while I drink a beer, and I can feel her tension from where I sit. It's part of my job as her dominant to keep an eye on her emotional wellbeing, and I can feel she's as tightly-wound as a taut spring.

"You okay?" I ask. I grasp the back of her neck with my fingers and give her a little squeeze.

"Better when you do that," she says with a sigh. I massage her neck and wait for her to talk. She lets out a breath. "I got edits back today, and I have some work to do. There are parts that are very strong," she smiles at me, "thank you for that. But there's a major plot hole I didn't see until my

JANE HENRY

editor gave me these edits back. It'll take hours and days to get it fixed."

"Well, I'll make sure you have that time," I tell her. "And it's also been a while since you've had a spanking."

Biting her lip, she wars with herself a bit before she responds. It's hard to admit she thrives under my firm discipline and guidance, but we both know it to be true. She's fully capable alone, and so am I, but together, we flourish.

If I let her go too long without being dominated, she gets irritable and feisty until I dom the hell out of her. Tonight's that night.

"Is there anything else on your mind?"

Her eyes don't meet mine. "Well," she begins. Her voice trails off, but I'm not letting this go. I wait for her to continue. Finally, with a sigh, she rolls her eyes and turns back to me. "It's stupid. The whole thing's so stupid."

"What?"

"I got an email from someone today. Someone who reads my books?"

"Yeah?"

"Yeah. They went on and on about how morally wrong my books are, because I have all these scenes where women are dominated, and books like mine have not only undermined the efforts of decades of feminist ideology and progress, they create weak-minded individuals who learn they have to depend on someone else to be fulfilled."

A clawing anger gnaws at my gut. I can hardly stand when she bangs her toe or has a headache;

hearing that someone treated her this way makes me want to punch a damn wall. "Is that right?" I ask, keeping my tone calm. "Well that's bullshit, and you know it."

"Do I?" she asks with a sad smile. "Yes, my books are fiction, but they're fantasy, too. I mean… it's what appeals to me. If I didn't like it, I wouldn't write it."

I take her hand. "You have full consent here."

"*Sometimes,*" she says. "I don't always like when you dom me."

I tug her onto my lap and hold her for a minute, feeling her settle against me. "Babe, that's not what consent is about. Sometimes you need me to take you beyond what's comfortable. The only way we ever grow is by pushing our limits. But you trust me, and that's your forte. You willingly give yourself over to me, and it takes incredibly strength to submit to someone else." I chuckle. "Hell, I couldn't do it."

She smiles. "You definitely do the 'in charge' thing better than the submission thing. It's just that, I wonder about morality sometimes. I hated that I was the one who tempted you from doing what was right so long ago. My parents berated me for it. The people in our town said I was a slut, that the good father never would have fallen from grace if it hadn't been for me. Just today, that stupid woman called me a *hussy*. God! I mean, in my heart, I know that you love me. And I love you. But sometimes, my head gets in the way and tells me I need to turn away from this."

I wrap my arms around her and hold her.

Sometimes, a submissive needs to question these things, and it's my job as her dom to listen, give her space to hash it all out, then help get her back on track. I don't have the doubts that she does. I accepted long ago that I was wired to dominate, that pursuing this lifestyle was the pinnacle of fulfillment for what I crave. I've long since forgiven myself for failing at my vows, for those vows were never meant for me.

"We'll leave the past in the past," I tell her. "And focus on the now."

She seems better now that she's gotten it off her chest, but before we can finish our conversation, Zack shoots me a text that gets my attention.

Meet me in Tobias' office?

When we arrive, he shuts the door behind us. "You two have a minute?"

I nod and pull out a seat for Chandra.

I feel a little guilty. I almost forgot about the investigation he's been doing, as to my knowledge there's been nothing else suspicious since that one night.

Tobias is at his desk, and Zack stands near Tobias with a folder in hand.

"I've done some investigating, and I've found a few things out," he says. "Does the name Fairwood Enterprises mean anything to you?"

I shake my head, and Chandra furrows her brow. "It's vaguely familiar, but I can't place it," she says. "But I haven't heard the name in years."

Zack pulls out some papers. "It's an organization run by the Bratva. One of their many sources of income, and their primary headquarters are in Atlanta."

This means nothing to me. I don't know anything about the Bratva or this organization, except some vague idea that it's organized crime.

"Well, it's weird," he says. "A bunch of our newest members have a history with the Russian military."

"Right." I remember he said that a few weeks ago.

"Recently, I found out we have an undercover agent who's been stationed with them for some time, and he's just relocated to NYC. I didn't know until yesterday and met with him last night."

"Someone I know?" I ask him.

Zack's jaw tightens. "I'm not at liberty to say. I'm sorry, but I'm bound to keep names and places confidential." But his eyes tell me a different story. Yes, it's someone I know and yes, he wants me to know. His voice lowers. "I won't confirm or deny. But think about it for a minute."

"Viktor." Chandra's face pales. "He mentioned his family's in Atlanta."

Zack shrugs a shoulder. It's confirmation enough.

"Nothing I say in here gets repeated outside of this office." He gives Chandra a stern look. "I mean *nothing.*" She and Marla are tight. I squeeze her hand and meet her eyes, underscoring Zack's admonition. She nods.

Zack continues. "The new members of the club are friendly with our agent, and I've confirmed they're all members of the Bratva. He knew they were coming here and made a play so he could join them. It goes without saying, we're not too keen on having members of organized crime in our club, but our informant says he is unaware of anything they've done since arriving. If they did, in fact, have anything to do with covering the surveillance cameras, he's unaware. His hands are tied being undercover."

"Of course."

"They're here funneling sources into their most lucrative business."

I fill in the blanks. "Fairwood Enterprises?"

Zack nods and blows out a breath. "And here's where you come in."

"Me?" I'm baffled.

"Yeah," he says. "You. Turns out Fairwood Enterprises was affiliated with a Sacred Heart church in a little town outside of Louisville. And according to my research, that was where you were stationed as a priest when you met Chandra."

A chill crawls down my spine. "Yeah," I confirm. "But it doesn't make any sense that a church has ties to the Bratva, Zack. C'mon. The diocese owns that property."

He shakes his head. "Not all of it. The town's archaic laws allowed bids to be placed on all property lots, so Fairwood Enterprises was, shall we say, the sponsor of Sacred Heart church. The diocese owns the actual *church*, but the rest of the property is owned by Fairwood."

I shake my head. We have Fairwood members right here, in Club Verge, and they're somehow connected to the church where Chandra and I met?"

"Yes. And my sources say because Fairwood Enterprises lost a significant amount of investments during the scandal, the Bratva's looking to capitalize on that."

I frown. "How?"

"Have you run into anyone you may have known?"

I shake my head but Chandra puts her hand on my arm. "We did," she says, her cheeks flushing. "Remember? At the mall?"

I look to Zack. "She was a cranky old bitch. How could she possibly be affiliated with the Bratva?"

Zack shrugs. "I'm not saying she is. But someone's looking for revenge, and sometimes those seeking revenge stop at nothing."

"What do they want from me?" I ask.

He shakes his head. "I have no idea." Sighing, he leans his elbows on his knees. "But honestly, I suspect someone working with the Bratva has hired them to seek revenge and nothing more."

"This is crazy, man. You think some old bitch is after me and Chandra because she lost her money in an investment?"

"I don't know," he says. "Give me her name and we run specs."

Chandra worries her lower lip. "Is…is Marla safe?" she asks.

"I'm not worried about Marla," Zack says. "She's with a dom now who will protect her." He clears his throat. He still doesn't want to name

Viktor, but we all know. Then he turns to Chandra. "But I'm not sure how far his protection goes. If he's distracted with Marla... It might be best for you to stay home from the bookstore until we've got this sorted."

Chandra lifts her chin with a defiant glare I know all too well. She's got a little brat in her that surfaces sometimes, and at the look she's giving me now, I know exactly what has to happen. My response to her is as instinctual as breathing.

"Chandra," I warn. That brings her eyes to me. I level a steady look at her and reach for her hand to let her know I'm listening to her and I won't take her away from what's important to her. By holding her hand, I can silently convey what I need to: a gentle squeeze to let her know I've got her, a firmer squeeze to warn her to behave before I have to punish her.

"This is my lifeline," she says to me. "I love working at the bookstore. Marla's my closest friend, and there's no way I'm going to let some trumped-up fear with literally no evidence to prove there's danger take me away from what I love."

I blink in surprise. She's being irrationally defiant, more so than I even expected.

"Chandra, listen," I begin, but she plows on as if I haven't said a thing.

"I don't mean to be disrespectful, Zack," she says, "I just don't see the need to change anything based on hardly any evidence. So, no, I'll still go to the bookstore, but I'll be careful."

Zack's jaw tightens, and he looks as if he wants

to say something, but he brings his eyes to mine and raises his brows. We communicate without words. He's asking me if I'm going to handle her, and I tell him with a firm nod as I get to my feet that I will.

"We'll talk about this privately," I say to Chandra, tugging her hand. I can feel her defiance radiating off her in waves. She wants to push back, maybe even has to, and she needs to know when she does I won't crumple. "I'll talk to you later, Zack."

Chandra doesn't say anything until we're out of the office. "Axle," she pleads. "This isn't fair. You can't just dom me into giving up everything that's important to me over the stupidest threat."

"We'll talk when we're alone," I tell her. I refuse to have this out here when I can't do exactly what I need to to stop her from spiraling out of control. I've heard enough from Zack that I believe him, and until his people have secured the possible threat to her, she'll stay safe if I have to spank her little ass every damn day and tie her to my bedpost.

"Axle," she fusses, trying to tug her hand out of mine but I only hold her hand firmer and walk faster. Finally, she gets the point, or at least she seems to, as she's now trotting along beside me instead of trying to get away. I scan the bar area but it's nearly vacant, only Travis wiping down the counter. He looks from me to her and knows exactly what's going on, so he just whistles to himself as if to say he's minding his own business. Good.

I finally get her to our private room, usher her in, and lock the door. I don't think of the room as just mine anymore. Girly toiletries and scents are littered throughout the bathroom, her shoes lined up in the closet, and backup changes of clothing neatly folded in the drawers. Other things I brought here myself also belong to her—a silky black blindfold, as well as a wooden paddle with the words *For Naughty Little Girls* emblazoned across the top. Though I prefer using my hands on her, and she prefers that, too, I got this one implement in the event of a punishment. She isn't rewarded with a hand spanking when she's naughty and knows I'm displeased when I take out the paddle.

I release her hand and point to her clothes. "Strip," I tell her.

But she doesn't submit as quickly as she should. Anchoring hands on her hips, she glares at me. I'm a little surprised by this. I knew she needed a spanking, but still, Chandra is naturally submissive, and it's rare she defies me so boldly.

"I want to talk first," she says, her body taut with anger, her eyes bright.

Frowning, I walk over to where we keep the implements with slow, purposeful strides. I know she's watching my every move. I want her fearing punishment and eventually, as our relationship progresses, she'll know my expectations, but she'll also grow to trust me more. She won't have as much of a need to defy me, and obedience will become intuitive.

Chandra knows she's in trouble. Good. I want her quaking a little inside, because a little fear before punishment will help. I wrap my hand around the sturdy handle of the paddle and cross my arms on my chest.

I watch as a little of her anger ebbs away when she looks at me, knowing now that I'm holding the paddle that she's crossed the line.

"Axle, no," she says, not defiant but pleading this time. "Not the paddle. Please, sir."

I shake my head, more convinced now than before that she needs me to light up her ass. If I back down now and let her go without a spanking, she might be superficially relieved, but a part of her will be disappointed. As a submissive, she craves this from me, and if I don't punish her when she defies me, she'll lose a little of the respect needed for this kind of relationship to work. But the paddle hurts. It's meant to. And she doesn't want a spanking.

I pull out the straight-backed chair I keep in our room for moments like these and sit heavily down. Wordlessly, I point to my knee. She captures her lips with her teeth, now looking far more apprehensive than angry. "Sir," she whispers.

"Dress up, over my knee."

"I want to talk."

I grit my teeth. "We'll talk with your dress up and you over my knee. Now you do what I say, or I'll double what you're already getting."

Watching her choose to submit is beautiful to me, the way she struggles and fights with her will, battling the conflict between what she wants and what she craves. But we weren't designed to be comfortable and complacent. I know the only way she'll grow is if she battles within and chooses to be strong, despite fearing the measured pain I'll give her. I grow in patience and fortitude when I give her the space to dance to this tune, to defy with the authenticity that doesn't break us but makes us stronger.

"I don't know about this," she says. "Maybe I don't want this. You're a little high handed."

"Chandra," I remind her, "When you're on the verge of getting your ass paddled is not the time to question our dynamic."

She pouts adorably with a little frown. "I think it's an excellent time to question."

Blowing out a shaky breath, she obeys, grabbing at the dress. Her eyes stay on mine, giving me her fear and apprehension along with her trust. I look at her steadily, not breaking eye contact, telling her without words what she needs to hear.

I expect you to obey.

I won't let you do this.

I love you.

She's so much happier when she's submitting to me, our dance of dominance and submission the passion that fuels who we are.

When she reaches me, I help her out of the rest of her clothes, then stand her in front of me naked. God, she's beautiful, I pull her between my legs and run my hands down her sides, over her soft skin, making her shiver. Leaning in, I kiss her softly, a promise that even though this part is hard, I love her.

"I love you," I remind her.

"And I love you," she says, and her eyes flash at

me. She's trying to behave, but there's a little devil in there that needs taming. "Even if you're an overbearing—"

She doesn't get a chance to finish, as I take her hand and guide her over my knee. Her beautiful curves beg to be punished, stroked, bitten, fucked, and seeing her bare-ass over my knee makes my cock swell. I want to bury myself in her so deeply she groans my name and forgets her own, plunge myself to the hilt and claim the deepest parts of her with savage, brutal, tender strokes. But first, a spanking is in order.

I rest the paddle on her naked rear. Adorably, one little hand flies up as if to block any smacks. I take her fingers with my left hand and press her fingers to her lower back.

"Keep them there, please," I admonish. "I don't want to strike your fingers with a paddle." Now that I'm holding her in position with the paddle ready to fly, we can talk.

"What did Zack ask you to do?" I don't spank her, not yet, just keep the paddle in place to remind her to behave.

"Not to go to the bookstore," she says, an air of resignation in her tone.

"Yes," I say, squeezing her hand just a little. "And what was your response?"

"I… I told him no, sir."

"And why is that?" I ask, feeling a bit of my anger return as we go over this. I'm looking forward to connecting the paddle with her ass. Hell, my dick pushes up against her soft belly in anticipation of that first solid smack, but first I'll give her the opportunity to give her side of the situation.

"I love my job sir," she says. Her hair hangs in beautiful swaths of glimmering chocolate brown. I release her hand just long enough to stroke my fingers through her long locks. I know she does, and I'm sympathetic to that.

"Go on."

"My entire life, I was told what to do," she says, her voice wobbling now. "I was told I couldn't do this, or I couldn't do that, and every rule was supposed to help me, but it didn't. It made me feel as if I had no autonomy at all, powerless and little. And I hated that."

She speaks the truth, but only in part. "Sweetheart," I tell her, brushing her hair off her forehead. "You were so strong, making your own way and fighting for what's yours. But this isn't about giving any of that up."

"It is!" she shouts. Frowning, I lift the paddle and bring it down with a good, firm whack against the fullest part of her ass. She yelps but settles a little over my knee and closes her mouth.

"It's childish and foolish to think that choosing safety in any way forfeits what you've worked so hard at," I tell her. "You *risk* your autonomy by making headstrong choices. If someone hurts you, you could lose freedom that will devastate you. And you're a smart girl, Chandra. You understand that."

She doesn't respond, and I'm not sure if she's being defiant or accepting what I say as truth, but I know how to bring that to light.

"You defied me. You refused to submit. And there are many things I'll compromise on, but your safety isn't one of them." It's all the warning I give her before I slam the paddle down hard on her bare ass. She arches her back and whimpers, but I continue with firm, unyielding strokes of the paddle. Five strokes in, she squirms. I know the sting builds with this paddle, and she wants it to end, but this punishment ends when she submits.

"I went for years without you," I tell her. "Years, I mourned the loss of you and gave up ever finding love again. No one could ever be *you.*" I spank her again. "You are the only one for me, and I'm not going to allow you to be foolish and do anything to harm yourself." I punctuate my words with sharp swats. "To take you from me. Or hurt you in any way." I spank her again.

"You're hurting me," she protests. I pause. She needs to fight me. She needs to know I won't cave.

"I'm spanking you," I clarify. "If I'm hurting you, you safeword." Her lack of response is all the answer I need to give me the green light to continue spanking her.

It takes four more firm, solid smacks, before I see a little bit of the fight go out of her. She no longer arches her back when the paddle connects but barely flinches. She's warmed up, her skin primed from the spanking and capable of taking more now, and she's sinking deeper into submission. Reaching for that place deep down inside her that gives her the power to yield to my authority. To accept correction.

To let herself be loved.

"You're not going back to work at the bookstore until I tell you," I explain, resting the paddle on her red-hot skin. "Will you?"

She shakes her head and speaks in a garbled voice. "No, sir."

"Good girl," I tell her. The paddle clangs to the floor but she doesn't even flinch, she's so deep into the moment, submerged in her submission. I take a moment to admire my handiwork and run my hand along her scorched, reddened skin. My cock pulses. There's nothing like a good, hard spanking that makes me want to fuck her more. My hand on her skin cues her in that her punishment is over. No more paddle. Just my hand. My fingers. My mouth.

"What are you going to do, Chandra?"

"Obey you, sir."

"Are you going to the bookstore?"

She sighs and shakes her head. "No, sir."

I massage her welted skin and nod my head. "Good girl. Is this forever, babygirl?"

"No, sir," she whispers with a sigh. She knows she was wrong. I just have to give her space to own that. "Just until you tell me it's safe again."

I continue the soothing strokes of my palm on her skin. "That's right. And is your only work at the bookstore anyway?"

"Well, no," she admits, squirming on my lap.

"What else do you do for work?"

"Write, sir."

"And will you be able to continue that?" I ask her, my hand resting on her ass.

She nods her head.

"You'll have ample time for writing, because you'll be staying with me and I'll be giving you plenty of time to do what you need to." I'm not sure yet what I'll do at the shop, but I'm taking on more hours at Verge and fewer at the shop, so I'll do what I need so that she's protected. "You can sit on my lap and work on your book or sit at the desk and write. I'll get you whatever you need to make that happen. Got it?"

She nods. "Got it, sir."

I catch a glimmer of dampness on her thighs and stroke my finger at the tender skin between her legs that's coated with arousal.

"Naughty girl," I pretend to chide. "Did you get turned on with a punishment?"

She shakes her head and bites her lip. "Not *during* the spanking," she begins. "It hurts too much."

But my words, my hands, my fingers on her now, bring us back to the inherent eroticism in what we do.

I pinch her thigh. "Open."

Her legs fly open. "That's it," I say. "Good girl. Maybe I won't punish you for getting turned on by a spanking, then," I say. "Maybe you deserve to climax."

"Yes, sir," she heaves out, opening her legs even wider. Her scent overwhelms me. I want to devour her. I *will*.

Chapter Fourteen

Chandra

"On the bed," he rasps out in a husky, sexy growl. My ass burns from the paddling he gave me, but the need to climax burns hotter. I wasn't even turned on when he paddled me. That paddle hurts like a bitch, and when Axle decides I need a spanking, he's all in. But when the pain stops and he's soothing me, my primed body yearns for his touch. He half carries, half drags me over to the bed, lifts me, and tosses me onto my back. I bounce a little. I know what he's going to do, and I can't breathe, I'm that caught up in anticipation.

"Pinch your nipples," he says, positioned at the foot of the bed. Obediently, I lift my hands to my chest and grab my own hardened nipples. My pussy pulses with need as he stands over me. Axle has many forms of aftercare and allowing me to come is one of my favorites.

"Remember your safeword," he tells me, before he kneels down in front of me, hovering his mouth over my sex. Hot breath caresses me like a gloved hand, my need ratcheting up with every breath he takes and releases. I want his mouth so badly my knees tremble and my breaths are labored, but he controls this just like he controls everything, devoted to meeting my every need, but too dedicated to my obedience to allow me to disobey. When I defy him, he disciplines me, and when I obey, I'm rewarded.

I took my spanking. It's reward time.

"You're beautiful," he breathes between my legs, the heat of his mouth pressing in on me.

"Thank you," I whisper, pulling my nipples harder. It's the only thing I can control here.

Then his mouth is on me and I'm breathless and writhing, sweet strokes of his tongue priming me to the point of release. I pinch harder and he strokes languidly, torturously slow then firmly pressing. I let go of my nipples so I can grasp his hair, but he crashes a hand against my thigh. I whimper when he takes his mouth off of me.

"Did I give you permission to stop?" he growls. I grab my nipples again and close my eyes as I'm soaring closer and closer to climax. When I'm just on the cusp he gets to his feet and strips. I'm trembling, on the edge of losing my mind, when he grabs my hands, pins them above my head, then drives his cock into me so hard I stop breathing. My mouth hangs open and my voice is garbled and strained when he thrusts again and again.

"Come for me," he orders. "Chase that climax, baby."

His words unleash what I need to let go, and I soar into my climax. My back arches, my heart races and my breath freezes as my body is wrecked with bliss at the same time that he lashes into me and grunts his pleasure. We climax long and hard, a crescendo of passion and power and love that courses through me and leaves me begging for more.

"I love you," he whispers.

"I love you," I whisper back. "God, I love you."

"You're incorrigible," he says. "I ought to paddle you morning and night just as insurance."

"Mmm," I moan, my eyes closed as I ride out the aftermath of that session. "No paddle."

"You really hate that thing."

"Tool of the devil."

"Good. Maybe it'll keep you in line for a little while."

I sigh and roll into him as he pulls me onto his chest, still connected, messy and sweaty but sated. "A little while," I whisper. "An hour or two. Maybe a few minutes."

"Maybe," he says, giving my ass a playful swat.

And as I come down from my high, what Zack told us comes back to me. A sadness presses in on my chest, and he must feel the change in me, for he mentions it.

"Something on your mind?"

I sigh. "Well. Yes, sir. I don't like remembering

what happened. I don't like remembering how they treated you. How they treated *us.*"

"Me neither," he admits. "And I wish there was something I could do about it, baby. All we can do is forget what happened and choose to live in the here and now. No one should have to put up with what you did. And if I have anything to do with it, no one ever will again."

I sigh. "I just—I have this horrible feeling like this is my fault. You were the good one, and I was the needy girl who—"

"Stop that." His harsh tone makes me freeze mid-sentence. "Don't you ever let me hear you say a thing like that again." He pauses to give weight to his words. "Where did this come from?" he asks.

"Well, seeing that woman there today. Hearing what she said, it just made me remember all the things my parents said. What the papers said. How they all painted me as this slutty temptress who persuaded the good man to fall. I was the classic Eve in the garden who handed you the apple."

"No, Chandra. We're not going there. What we did was in the past, and even though we did things we shouldn't have, we're making this right now."

I frown, and suddenly in my vulnerable state, all my doubts are coming at me full force. "By playing dom and sub at a BDSM club? This is somehow right and good?"

I don't like the way his eyes flash at me, and I know I'm pushing things too far, but I need to state my fears and have him resolve those. I need to know that this is okay.

———————

We lay together in the quiet neither one of us speaking after my revelations. Outside our private room are muffled sounds of play, but in here, there's only our heartbeats and breathing. I reach for his hand and weave my fingers through his, when a knock sounds at the door. Gesturing for me to stay put, he gets out of bed and covers me with a blanket so whoever's at the door doesn't see me naked. He looks around for his jeans, but we've left our clothes strewn about the room. He swears under his breath and yanks open his dresser door. "Just a minute," he barks at the door, tugging the jeans on.

He goes to the door and creaks it open then has a brief, hushed conversation. I try to see who's there but can only see Axle's broad, muscled back, but it surprises me that it's a female voice. Who's he talking to, and why is it okay for them to interrupt us?

Frowning, I push myself to sitting, trying to get a good look, but I can't see anything. Finally, he shuts the door and turns to me.

"I gotta step out for a minute," he says. "I want you to stay here for now."

"Is everything okay?" I don't like this at all.

Shrugging a shoulder, he frowns. "I'm not sure. But right now, you need a little down time and quiet, and I can't watch you the way I'd like to out there. So just stay here until I come back for you. Got it?"

My heart sinks, but I'm determined not to let him down. Not again. I'm feeling little and vulnerable, alone like this, and I know in my gut I need some aftercare. Some attention, but I don't speak up. "Got it."

Before he leaves, he bends down and gives me a sweet, lingering kiss that makes me arch right up off the bed and into him. "Rest, baby," he says. "I need to check on a few things. We need to make sure everyone's safe here." And then he's back at his dresser and pulling on a rumpled, faded black t-shirt. I smile at the irony. He may have chosen a different path than he planned, but he's still a good man. I watch him leave, and sigh to myself.

I flop back onto the bed and sigh, pulling the covers up over my shoulder. To pass the time, I pick up my phone and scroll through. There's a message from Marla.

Dinner tonight with Viktor and some of his friends, then we're heading into the club. Will you be there?

Viktor's friends? Something tells me not to trust these guys. Zack practically said they're members of the Bratva. I do a search for *Bratva* and feel my eyes go wide at the results.

Organized crime.

Former Soviet Union.

Powerful, ruthless.

If these men are who Zack fears they are, they're right here, infiltrating this club, and there's nothing we can do about it until the undercover agent or agents bring them down. I hate the idea of my friend being in such close proximity. Quickly, I text her back.

Marla, can you meet me at the club sooner? There are some things I need to talk to you about, and I don't want to be overheard.

Her response comes quickly.

I'm sorry, I'm already heading to the restaurant. I'll get there as soon as I can.

Ugh. My friend is wining and dining with people who could hurt her. Kill her. I need to do something. But what?

I shoot Axle a text. *I need to see you.*

Axle told me to stay but I need to warn Marla. Maybe if I find him, he can help me in a way that doesn't compromise anyone's safety. I push myself out of bed and feel the burning sting of the paddle with every move that I make. Damn, he spanked me good. I'll feel that one for days. Opening the drawers where I keep my clothes, I choose one of the outfits Axle's picked out for me and slip it on.

What am I doing? I allowed him to spank me. I'm wearing the clothes that he bought and staying in this room because he told me to. Why do I like this?

Do I like this?

I need to talk to him. He told me to stay here, but he's been gone a while, and it doesn't matter anyway. If he really loves me, he'll love me without the trappings of a lifestyle like this. Maybe I need a little space. I'm strong and capable, and I'm not sure I need to submit to him to prove that.

I stand and go to retrieve my clothes when I notice a folded square of paper on the floor. I bend to pick it up. It must've fallen to the ground when he took his clothes out. When I read the words, a chill rolls over my body. The note's written in a swirly script with hearts dotted over the "i's."

Sir, thank you for everything you've done. Love, Missy

What the hell is this? I crinkle it up and toss it back to the floor.

After dressing, I glance at my phone again, but there's nothing. He hasn't responded. With my hand trembling, I push open the door. I don't like disobeying him, but our relationship should be stronger than obedience and rules.

I feel a little like a child sneaking out of bed at night when I walk down the hall. My ass burns from the spanking he gave me, and I know that it doesn't matter if he just spanked me or not, if he catches me out here, he'll reignite that sting pretty damn easily.

If I let him, that is. Maybe I won't let him.

The hall is vacant, but the dungeon is filled to the brim, couples scening and mingling and socializing. Every bit of the furniture is occupied, and there's even a line at some places where people are waiting their turn. Someone's suspended in a harness, and several dungeon monitors pace the floor. I recognize a man named Geoffrey as well as Braxton and Zack. I know Brax and Zack are there for a reason: they're on the lookout for any signs of danger.

It's dark in here and there's some kind of smoke machine tonight. Zack walks over and has a hushed conversation with someone, gesturing to the machine, but the man shakes his head. And then I see him. Axle's standing with a woman at the far end of the room, hidden in shadows and smoke, but I see the tattoos along his arm and the same black t-shirt he wore when he left the room. I blink in confusion. He's not checking on things to make sure they're okay. He's... holding a woman on his arm. I stare at them, so confused and shocked I don't know what to do when I see him lean down and kiss the pretty woman, lingering and sexy. My heart cracks like shattered crystal, shards of hopes and dreams crashing down around me.

I take a step toward them and freeze. Do I want him to see me?

He wouldn't. He *couldn't*. How could he?

Is that "Missy" he's with?

I trusted him. I loved him. I love him, still. Is this why he demanded I stay in the room? So that he could meet with his other woman? I shake my head. This can't be happening. This isn't happening.

We went too fast, too soon. I should have taken my time with getting to know him. He isn't who I once knew, and I rushed in too soon. God, I'm stupid. I'm so damn stupid. I don't know if I want to laugh or cry or tear him away from her like a jealous, vengeful lover. My blood turns to liquid lava, molten hot, and I clench my fists.

I don't know what to do with myself. If I leave Verge now, I abandon Marla to the fucking *mafia*, and if I stay, he'll see I left the room. With my head unfocused and dizzy and my heart shattered into pieces, I make my way to the bar. I'll have a drink and not talk to anyone and figure out a way to make this better. Sliding onto a stool, I lift a hand in greeting to Travis. I breathe a sigh of relief when he pours me my usual and pushes it across the counter.

"How many are you allowed tonight?" he asks, politely but with the hint of his natural domly-ness.

I lift the drink and take a long, deep pull from it before I answer him. "As many as I want." It doesn't feel good saying that, though, and the curious look he gives me doesn't appease my conscience.

I need to talk to Axle. Frowning, I pick up my phone. I send him a one-word text.

Mad.

I feel sick.

I take another sip of my drink to quell my rising nerves and soothe the ache in my heart. I waited for years for him. For years. I told myself that everything I did was to create a new me, to leave behind the shattered past and create a new present. When I found him, I felt as if the stars aligned and my hopes and dreams would finally come to fruition. No one loves me the way he does, with the tender, loving care that only years of history can bring, as we've forged our way through heartache and misery. We've earned our happiness, and it feels so wrong that it's been ripped away from us so soon. How could he?

My phone beeps with a text. When I read it, my skin prickles with nerves and anger.

Axle: Meet me in the dungeon. By the loveseat. Kneel and wait for me.

Did he ignore my safeword?

Glaring at my phone, I text again. *Mad.*

Axle: Dungeon. Loveseat. Kneeling.

Maybe he wants to talk. The last "talk" we had was with his paddle on my ass, so apparently, he wants to talk on his terms.

My heart twists in my chest and I swallow down the lump the size of a brick. God. I don't want to believe he betrayed me. Fine. I'll do what he says, but I'll have plenty to say to him.

Chapter Fifteen

Axle

I leave the dungeon and come back to the private room, but to my shock, when I push open the door, she's gone.

Gone.

"Chandra?" I'm half angry, half concerned. I gave her a specific instruction and it's unlike her to disobey me. Especially, after a spanking. Where has she gone?

The bed's unmade, but otherwise the room looks exactly the way it did before I left it. I reach into my pocket to pull out my phone to shoot her a text but find that my pocket's empty. What the hell?

My gut clenches. Something's wrong.

I head to the dungeon at a trot and practically crash into Marla. "Hey," she says, her brows furrowed. "Have you seen Chandra?"

"I was just about to ask you that," I tell her.

She shakes her head. "It's the weirdest thing. I was at the store and one of Viktor's friends said they had plans to go out with us. There must've been some confusion because when I talked to him, he had no clue." She frowns and looks a little sad. "When he found out, he was upset. He told me never to make plans without consulting him first. I mean, I get it…" Her voice trails off and she worries her lip. If my suspicion is correct, I know exactly why he was furious. He's undercover, and the Bratva he's tracking went behind his back and made plans with his girl. Not good.

"What did he tell you?" I ask her.

"He said he was on his way to me. He knew I was coming here." She frowns. "It was so weird. He said go straight to Zack and don't talk to anyone else."

I cross my arms on my chest. Dammit, why doesn't anyone listen? "And yet you're standing here talking to me."

"Well, I'm trying to find Chandra," she said. "Axle, what the hell is going on?"

"Your dom gave you an instruction," I tell her. "Let's find Zack. And I have no idea where Chandra is."

Marla flushes, abashed, and swallows. "Yeah," she says. "I'll find Zack. Why did Chandra text me earlier? She asked me to come here and said there was something she needed to talk to me about."

What? I shake my head. "I have no idea." I run a hand through my hair. I know I left her after a scene with no aftercare, but I came out because Tobias had some concerns he wanted to go over with me. The men Zack suspect are here, tonight, and we don't know exactly how many of them there are. He wants me and Zack to track them down and keep an eye on them to make sure they don't make any moves.

"Marla. Zack," I order.

We need to get control of this. Things are beginning to spiral out of control, and I don't like this, not at all.

She leaves and heads to Zack. I want to talk to him myself, but for now I need to find Chandra and when I do, I'll punish her for disobeying me. God. I thought I'd made my point loud and clear earlier. Apparently not.

I'm going to scour every inch of this place until I find her. I leave the dungeon and head to the private room. I make sure one more time it's empty and look around for any clues that might tip me off to where she's gone, but all I see is a crumpled piece of paper that's fallen to the floor. I pick it up and unfold it, frowning at the words that look almost foreign.

Sir, thank you for everything you've done. Love, Missy

It takes me a minute to even realize where this note came from, then I remember. It must be four or five years old. I probably tossed it on the dresser and it fell into the drawer, because I haven't known anyone by the name of Missy for a long time. Furrowing my brow, I think. I have a vague memory of a petite college-aged girl who came in here before she moved away. She needed someone to talk to, and there were a few nights we scened together, but it was nothing serious at all. I toss the paper into the trash.

Did Chandra see this and get the wrong idea? I need to find her. We need to talk.Did she leave? *Jesus.*

I go back to the dungeon and find Zack. When I see him, he gives me a chin lift and flags me down.

"Gotta talk," Zack says, as soon as I reach him.

"Yeah, man. Me, too. You first."

He pulls out his phone and opens up a file. "Names and faces," he says. He can't say much in public with everyone here, though, so he has to be discreet. "Three here tonight."

I shake my head. "You confirmed this?"

"Yep. One by the spanking bench at ten o'clock, one by the pool tables, one just walked in."

I don't look, because I don't want to draw suspicion. I'll be looking for them, though. I'll fucking tail their asses. But I need to find Chandra.

"Listen," I tell him. I explain to him about Chandra leaving, the note I found, and the fact that my phone's gone and when I'm talking my adrenaline pumps, my heartbeat racing. Something's off, and I'm worried about Chandra.

"I don't like the fact that your phone's gone," he says in a low voice only I can hear. "And I came in here and the fucking smoke machine's going. I told them to shut it off, but they say they have instructions from Tobias and I haven't been able to reach him. Can't see a fucking thing." He shakes his head. "If the wrong person has your phone, they could text her pretending to be you."

Fuck. Damnit.

I look around the room, trying desperately to find her, but it's too hard to see anything and there are way more people than I'm used to. Outside this room a commotion breaks out by the bar area, and the walkie talkie Zack carries on DM nights sounds. He hits a button and Travis's voice comes through.

"Fight by the pool tables," he says. The walkie talkie clatters down and I figure Travis has gone to break it up. Zack shakes his head. "Keep an eye on things in here," he says, and he leaves.

I hear a scream behind me and turn to see a man lighting into a woman. She's bound and cuffed to the whipping post and he's plying the whip so hard it makes even me cringe, and I've seen a fuck ton of intense scenes. *Jesus.* I can't interfere, though, not unless I have reason to believe he's taking advantage of her. Members take things far here, sometimes, and it's my job as DM not only to not interfere, but make sure no one else does.

And I need to find Chandra. On my way over to stand by the whipping post, though, I hear a cry that's all too familiar to my ears. I scan the room, dim and clouded with smoke, but I'd recognize

JANE HENRY

that hair, the curve of her shoulders and sweet face knelt insubmission. It's Chandra. She's cuffed and gagged and kneeling by a bench, and there's a man standing right next to her. A chill runs over me. He's my height, covered in tats, and wearing the same t-shirt I am. I take off at a run.

Chapter Sixteen

Chandra

I came in here as I was instructed and knelt by the bench, but I didn't see Axle. I need to talk to him. I have to see him. We need to figure out what's going on. I'm tender and afraid, and I need Axle.

And then I see him, standing a good distance away. I recognize his t-shirt but before he comes any closer, he snaps his fingers and points to the ground, an indication for me to look down. I don't at first. I'm angry at him. But he does it again, and I don't want to begin with him angry at *me* or we'll never be able to talk.

I look down. I'll obey first, and then we'll talk.

When he reaches me, I'm staring at the floor, and something feels off. He doesn't touch me. He doesn't speak. But a silky gag glides over my mouth and I feel him cinch it at the back of my head. I move my head to look at him but a blindfold slips over my eyes and a low whisper's at my ear.

"You do what I say and come with me to our room."

This is wrong. Something's wrong. I texted him my safeword and yet he's scening with me. Something cold and hard brushes my wrists. He's cuffing me. Why is he cuffing me?

I try to speak but I'm gagged so I can't. My heart races and I try to pull away from him but he's yanking me to my feet. Is this even Axle? My Axle doesn't handle me roughly like this. He never gags me. And he would listen to me if I safeworded.

But my Axle doesn't talk to other women, either.

The blindfold dampens with my tears of frustration, and he's pulling me, dragging me out of here. I stumble, and he lifts me up, but he doesn't tuck me against his chest. He's holding me in his arms like I'm deadweight, and he's moving *fast*. I'm struggling against him and I'm screaming against my gag, but it's muffled and garbled.

I hear someone shouting. I stop moving. I don't say anything. The voice comes at a distance and it's Axle.

I writhe against the man carrying me. If that's Axle's voice, who the hell is this? I push, trying to get away, but he's so strong, he's hurting me. Then everything explodes in confusion. Behind me someone screams in pain and agony and I don't know if it's just a dungeon scream or worse, then I'm torn from the arms of the man carrying me.

Someone's wrestling whoever has me and in the midst of confusion, I hear Axle shouting for them to let me go. I fall, hit my head, and everything goes black.

———

My head feels heavy. So heavy. Where am I? I try to open my eyes, but they feel so heavy. Murmured voices come from above me and beside me and I drift back off to sleep, in and out of consciousness. When I wake again, it's quiet. So quiet. My head hurts so painfully my stomach clenches. I open my eyes with effort. There's blinding white light all around me. I'm in a narrow hospital bed with a white sheet pulled up over me. I sit up with a start, then Axle's by my side.

"Easy, baby," he says. "You've got a nasty concussion. Lay back down."

I want to relax at the sound of his voice. I want to listen to him. But he's the man who betrayed me. Still, I need to find out what's going on, so even though I watch him with a guarded look, I lay back down.

"Where am I?" I whisper.

"The hospital," he says. "You got injured at the club and we had to bring you here." His eyes are bloodshot and he's wearing the same clothes he wore the last time I saw him.

"How long have I been here?"

He reaches over and takes my hand. "About six hours. It's early morning, and Zack's on his way in."

"What happened?"

He sighs, lets go of my hand, and goes to shut the door. "Let's wait until Zack gets here to fill us in. For now, I want to hear your side of the story." He sits back down and reaches for my hand, but when he reminds me of the night before, I refuse to take it.

"I stayed in the room waiting for you," I tell him. "And… well, I was having some reservations about things." I tell him as he watches me without a word. "I went to get dressed and found a note written to you by *Missy.*" His eyes darken but he still says nothing. "I went out to the dungeon and saw you kiss a woman."

"Bullshit."

My heart wants it to be false. I want to believe him. I need to.

"There's no way," he says. "For Christ's sake, Chandra, don't you know by now I'd never be with another woman?"

"I know," I say, a lump rising in my throat. I try to swallow it, but I can't. It dissolves, and a tear rolls down my cheek. "But it looked just like you."

"And that's something we'll have to discuss with Zack."

Swallowing, I continue. "So I went to the bar and had a drink but before I could speak to you, and I… I safeworded. But you texted and instructed me to kneel and wait for you in the dungeon."

I'm afraid he's going to find something and break it, pound the wall with his fist, or roar like a savage animal, the look in his eyes is so feral.

"Then things got confusing, though. I followed your instructions, but you were acting strangely."

"Of course, because it wasn't me."

I sigh. God. I was played for a fool. I have no idea why, but everything spiraled out of control. A knock sounds at the door and Zack walks in, but he's not alone. Viktor walks in beside him, looking tired and wan with a swollen lip and black eye. I wait. I need to know what happened but even though my head pounds, my heart is hopeful. It wasn't him. Something was amiss, and we'll figure that out, but he didn't cheat on me. He wouldn't. God, I was stupid.

Viktor reaches a hand to me. "Agent Ivanov," he says. "Undercover agent. What we say in this room is highly confidential. Even Marla will not know. She will, eventually, but not yet."

Axle gives me a look that underscores this command. I nod as Viktor and Zack take seats.

"About a month ago, I came here following a small circle of men who were hired to hurt Axle. It was a professional hire and was supposed to end with a hit."

I blink. What?

"Why?" I ask.

"Seven years ago, as you know, Axle was a Father Noah at a small church in Louisville. There were several rich parishioners who invested in the property affiliated with Fairwood Enterprises. When the…" he pauses and looks apologetically at Axle, "scandal went down, investors pulled out. And a certain investor, Veronica Vanderkilt, invested so much, she went into financial ruin."

"Oh my God," I whisper.

He shakes his head. "It wasn't your fault. The investments were stacked illegally, funded by the Bratva, and when the deals fell through, the investors were scrambling. So, she's been trying to track Axle, and it appears she did so out of pure revenge. She hired the men who were at the club last night, and they were happy to oblige, since their investments were tied into the church as well."

"This is crazy," I say. He nods and shrugs, not disagreeing with me.

"I knew the plan, but I couldn't act right away. I'm still undercover with them. They're heading back to Atlanta, and I'll have to join them in the morning." He continues, his eyes going from me to Axle. "Their plan was to take you," he says. "But the plan was sloppy and poorly orchestrated. One dressed like Axle, and someone stole his phone. They were staging a kidnapping. Zack's men have uncovered the van in the back parking lot of Verge, ready to take you. They were planning on Axle following, and the plan then was to stage his execution. But their plan was sloppy. They began with a staged fight in the bar area to distract Zack, but Travis ended that too quickly, and then there was supposed to be a second man there to perform the abduction." He smiles. "That man was supposed to be me. I pretended to be dealing with Marla, and I never arrived in the dungeon. As you know, Axle intervened, and the rest is history."

"You got beat up over it?" I ask.

Viktor shrugs. "I have men in high places," he says. "It ended quickly."

"And now what?" Axle asks.

Viktor sighs. "The Bratva left, and they're heading back to Atlanta. They're powerful and slippery. Once they're gone, they're gone. I'll be joining them, but I needed to talk to you two first." He gets to his feet.

"Marla knows nothing?" I ask.

He shakes his head. "Not yet. All she knows is that there's a family emergency and I'm heading home. It's safer for her this way, Chandra." And then he's on his feet and shaking our hands, before he leaves. Zack talks to Axle, but I lay back on the bed, stunned and quiet. This could've gone so terribly, terribly wrong.

Finally, we're alone. And I want to cry.

The door clicks shut, and Axle's got me in his arms. He's on the bed and holding me and everything is right again.

"I was so confused," I tell him. "I saw the note and my head was all a jumble. Then when I saw you with her—"

"Shh," he says. "I left you after an intense session. You weren't in your right frame of mind. You needed a good, long, aftercare session."

"Yeah," I say. "I should've known you would never do that."

"Of course, I wouldn't." We sit in the silence, my head on his shoulder.

"Will they do anything else to hurt us?" I ask.

He shakes his head. "Viktor says they moved on. Correction. Our *source* says they moved on. We don't know anything." His voice takes on a stern edge when he raises a brow at me. "Understood?"

I nod.

"At first, our source wasn't sure if they'd pursue us or not, but he diverted their attention with another job. Now he's making sure they do everything they can to focus on that."

"So we're safe?"

He nods, though he looks a bit apprehensive. My guess is that we're fine, but Viktor isn't out of the woods.

"He's at risk," I whisper. "If they find out—"

"You let him worry about that."

I close my mouth and just let myself obey. It feels nice. God, it feels so damn nice.

"And Missy? Who's Missy?" I ask.

He shrugs. "I knew her years ago. We didn't even date. She left me a note when I helped her out, and it must've been in my dresser." His tone hardens. "Chandra, you have questions, you *ask* me. Do you understand? God, I should punish you just for doubting us."

I sigh. "I'm sorry, sir. I will. I promise."

When he squeezes me, my heart throbs in tune with his. My head hurts and my body's sore, but my heart is at peace. He never betrayed me.

"Good girl," he says with the whisper of a kiss on my forehead. "Such a good girl. We're going to leave this place, and we're moving in together."

He's not asking, but I don't care. I love when he commands things. I love when he's the one in charge like this.

"Yes," I whisper. It's right. So damn right.

"When I know things are safe at the club, we can go back, but for now you're with me. And when the weather warms up, we'll get married in a little chapel in the city. Just a small ceremony."

I smile. "Yes, sir. Let's do that."

My heart is filled to bursting. I was silly and foolish, but he doesn't blame me like he could have. Because he loves me. I was meant to be his, and he belongs to me.

"I want to wake up every day with you by my side and tuck you in beside me when I go to bed at night. I want you to wear my ring and make vows that are right and good. The ones I was meant to make. To love, honor, and protect you. Because I love you."

"And I love you," I whisper. "God, I love you so much."

This time, things are right. We were lost and broken, but now we're saved. We'll face sadness and happiness, wins and losses. But in the end, we'll emerge from the ashes, stronger and more powerful, together as one. Sometimes we need to fall and get back up again and keep on going. Sometimes terrible, painful tragedy strikes, but we're forged in that fire. And we keep on. Maybe we're scathed and maybe we hurt, but in the end, we remain victorious.

Because in the end we love, and we are loved.

Epilogue

"Keep your hands where I put them, and do not move."

"Yes, sir."

I lean in and grip Chandra's hair, tug her head back, and bring my mouth to her ear. "He's got her well-trained, doesn't he?"

We're sitting on a loveseat in the dungeon, and Viktor's got Marla trussed up and at the mercy of his crop. Her eyes glow, her cheeks flushed, and she's the perfect image of a submissive in utter bliss at the hands of a dom she trusts.

"Oh, he tries," Chandra says, squirming on my lap on purpose. "But he's got a long way to go with that girl." She knows when she wiggles her lap on my ass it makes me hard, which is exactly what she wants. I slap the side of her full thigh and pull her hair a little tighter.

"And if I didn't know any better, I'd suspect he doesn't really want to train her fully anyway."

"Too true."

Zack won't confirm or deny whether or not Viktor still works undercover for the Bratva, but I've noticed in the past year his face has thinned and his eyes are rimmed with dark circles. If the man's still undercover, it's eating him up. I hope he's relieved of his job soon, and before the toll his job takes is irreparable.

Marla's sharp cry interrupts our conversation when Viktor plies the crop harder, the swish and thud making my dick thicken. I want that crop in my hand. I want that ass on display to be Chandra's.

I need to get her alone. My plans for her don't involve anyone's eyes but mine.

"Time for us to go," I say to her. She met me here after work and may have been hoping to scene tonight. But what we have at our own place awaits.

One of my customers at the shop gave me a deal on a high-rise not ten minutes away from the bookstore and Verge, and we've been there now for a while. Chandra has an office in the library, books piled so high on every shelf she's dwarfed by them, a comfy desk chair, and a couch to sit and type on if she feels like it, but many times, she sits on my lap at night and writes. I watch TV or read a book and she snuggles in and types away. She says being near me inspires her. I don't know anything about writing, but I do know this: if anyone's inspiring anyone, she's the one doing the inspiring.

When I wake with her by my side, I say a prayer of thanksgiving for the beauty she brings into my life. When I hold her in my arms, I praise the sweet feel of her soft curves beneath my hands, the body that responds so well to me, she tells me without words that we were made for each other. When I inhale her scent and feel her warm hand in mine, I cherish the second chance we've been given and vow that I'll never take any of this for granted. When I kiss her full, sultry mouth, and slide my hands along the silky small of her back, I venerate the beauty that belongs to me. *Mine. All mine.*

But now it's time to take things to the next level.

We leave Verge and head home and she chatters away about work for a while. Her books are sailing to the top of the lists, and her readership is growing. Last week she had a book signing, and next week she's doing an interview for some magazine. I love to see her thriving at what she loves, and I'll do whatever I need to so that she never loses that passion.

I listen as she changes the subject and chatters about the fish she bought, all set up in an aquarium in our dining area. They're exotic fish from all over the world, and it's adorable how excited she gets about them. She spent as many hours naming them as she did researching the proper water temperature, filtration, and feeding.

When we reach our apartment, I smile at her. "You'll be a good mom," I tell her, tweaking her nose. I push the button on the elevator that takes us upstairs.

That makes her sober a bit. "Anyone can feed

fish," she says sadly. "But babies? I don't know." And her eyes grow a little sad and wistful, the way they always do when I say anything that reminds her of the baby she lost. *We* lost.

"I do know," I tell her. We ride in silence to our apartment. She's quiet and contemplative when I open the door, her thoughts otherwise occupied.

I shut and lock the door while she checks on the fish and talks to them. I smile with my back to her so she doesn't see how ridiculous I think her little routine is when she talks to the damn fish on the other side of the glass.

"Did you have a good day?" she asks. "Get a good nap in? Discover any secret passages? My day was good, but a certain someone," she gives me a sidelong look, "decided to take me home before we had any fun."

"Keep it up and that fun will turn into your little ass bared over my knee," I tell her, eyeing her with firm warning. "No pouting, baby."

She sighs and turns back to the fish. If we had plants, she'd talk to them, too, and I'd fucking love it. Christ, I love everything about her.

"Chandra," I say from our bedroom a few minutes later, when I'm ready for her. "Come here, please." It takes effort to keep my voice steady. My hands are a hopeless cause. They shake in anticipation, my heart thudding so madly in my chest I wonder if she can hear me. I hear her say good-bye to her fish, then she makes her way to me. I want to capture this moment in my mind forever. I never want to forget the way she looks when she knows what I'm about to do.

When she comes into the room, she pauses in the doorway. The flicker of the candles on the bedside tables reflect in her eyes, wide open with wonder. She brings her hand up, and her fingers delicately cover her mouth in surprise.

"Axle?" she whispers. "What…is this?"

Nothing but candlelight illuminates the room, but it's enough that she can see the large vases teeming with crimson and white roses. I had so many delivered the whole room's infused with the enchanting floral scent. Earlier when she was at the bookstore, I put all this in place so I was ready. Now, I just focus on her.

"It's the next step," I tell her. I swallow so my voice carries clear and strong across the room. I don't want it to waver. I want her to know now and forever that I mean what I say. When I draw the small black velvet box from my pocket, her luminous eyes fill with unshed tears and I have to swallow that damn lump in my throat again.

The soft flicker of candlelight. Her breathing and mine. The silent question that hangs before us, and the answer that will change the course of our lives forever.

"You know, a part of me's still pretty damn traditional," trying to make light of this, but when I drop to one knee and she sniffs, I have to take in a deep breath.

"I lost you once, Chandra. And now I have you back. I don't ever want to lose you again." I open the box. The diamond I chose glitters in the candlelight. She gasps. "I want you by my side for the rest of my life. I want to raise children with you. I want to see you grow and flourish into the woman you were always meant to become, and I want to be the man that is with you every step of the way."

She walks over to me on trembling legs. I hold the ring up to her and meet her eyes.

Now that I've begun, my voice holds strong and confident. "Will you marry me?"

When she blinks, one tear rolls down her cheek. "Yes. Yes! I will marry you. I want all those things too." To my surprise, she kneels beside me and places her forehead on my shoulder. "I feel the same. I don't ever want to be apart from you again."

Four months later

We don't believe in long engagements. "We waited this long," I tell her, and she finishes, "we don't need to wait any longer."

We say our vows in a little chapel tucked away amidst the hustle and bustle of the city, attended only by our closest club friends as witnesses. I said vows once before, but I've forgiven myself for the sins I've committed. Sometimes our paths take twists and turns we don't expect. Sometimes, the plans that we lay go astray.

For years, I prayed for forgiveness. And the

answer to that prayer holds my hands while I slip a ring on her finger.

She's every bit the princess in a gorgeous white dress she calls a "sheath" dress but I don't care what she calls it. A dress is a dress, and today, Chandra becomes my wife. That's all that matters.

After the ceremony, we sip champagne and eat food, but I don't remember what we ate or what was said. My sole focus was on her. The way her musical laugh lights up the room around us. The way she sits with her head on my shoulder and reaches for my hand when Marla gives a toast that has everyone in the room wiping away tears. The way her cheeks blush when I whisper what I plan to do to my wife when I get her alone.

My wife.

Six months later

"Baby?" I open the door to our apartment and look for her but don't hear her at first. Then her muffled voice comes from the bathroom.

"In here," she says, but her voice is barely audible. I go to her, concerned that she doesn't sound so good.

"Chandra, you alright?" I ask at the door.

"Come in," she groans. Heartbeat pounding, I open the door. She's kneeling, her arm resting against the toilet seat, one arm resting against her forehead.

"What's the matter, honey?" I ask her, kneeling beside her. "Trying to recreate our reunion?"

She laughs her musical laugh and gives me a watery smile.

"Sure," she says. "Let's go with that."

I brush her damp hair off her forehead and kiss her temple. "Can I get you anything?"

Leaning back so she's sitting on her feet, her hands dropped onto her lap, she nods. "Yes, please. On that shelf up there? Right next to the sink? Hand it to me?"

For some reason she doesn't meet my eyes. Curious, I reach for the shelf and freeze when my hand meets a thin white stick. I know what it is before I see the two pink lines in the little windows.

I drop to my knees in front of her. I don't trust myself to speak. She needs me to be strong and I'm gonna lose my shit if I open my mouth right now.

"April," she whispers. "Right around Easter."

Spring. New hope. New life. A new beginning.

"Baby," I whisper, gathering her up in my arms.

"Yes," she says with a laugh. "A baby."

"Don't you think for a minute this means you don't get your ass spanked now," I tease her. "Every study I've ever read tells us pregnancy doesn't change much." There are a few things. Lighter implements. Less impact play. But there's plenty we can do.

"And don't you think for a minute that just

because I'm pregnant I don't need you to dom me."

I grip her hair and pull. "Deal." Her mouth parts when I pull her head back.

"I love you," she says.

"And I love you," I whisper. "I loved you then and I love you now, and I'll love you until the day I die."

I hold her to me. She's my light and my hope. My everything and I will cherish her forever.

I regretted the vows I made and broke. I carried my cursed around like a yoke on my shoulders. But now? Now, I vow with everything in me that I will love and cherish Chandra until the day I die. I love her more with every day that passes.

My heart sings poetic when she looks up at me.

"Soul meets soul," I whisper, my favorite poem.

"On lovers' lips," she finishes.

I smile and lean into the kiss.

THE END

Also by Jane Henry

Need more NYC Doms?

Although each book is a stand-alone novel and can be
read in any order, the chronological order is as follows:

Deliverance

He's bred to protect.

Tobias Creed likes things done his way, and he likes his
women ready to submit. No strings attached. Until the
night he meets the one woman who challenges him,
practically begging to be taken over his knee.

As a single mom to a child with special needs, Diana McAdams does things her way. She's in control and doesn't have time for love. Happily-ever-afters aren't for her.

Then she meets the man who demands her submission...

Read more

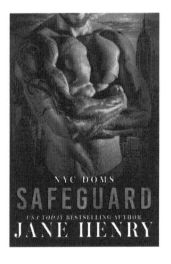

Safeguard

She's feisty, gorgeous, impossible.

Submissive.

And all mine.

I don't do half-assed relationships. When I set my sights

on the most headstrong, tenacious submissive I've ever met, I'm all in. I'll show her the dark, sensual world she craves, dominate her, and leave her begging for more. But when her safety's endangered, she needs more than a dom: she needs a safeguard.

Read more

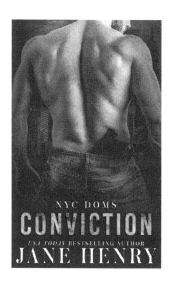

Conviction

Braxton Cannon can't get the girl on the dance floor out of his mind, the woman he literally swept off her feet and into Club Verge.

She's no submissive, but he can't help but admire her ferocity, even as he yearns to take her over his lap and teach her manners. He's determined to keep her safe if he has to lock her up himself.

Officer Zoe Mackay can handle herself. But when she learns information that puts her life at risk, she's forced to seek the assistance of a private investigator. Little does she know the man she hires is none other than Braxton Cannon, the high-handed dominant who gave her the hottest one-night stand of her life. With her assailants in hot pursuit, Zoe is forced to seek refuge in Club Verge, where she finds way more than she's bargained for…

Read more

About the Author

USA Today bestselling author Jane Henry pens stern but loving alpha heroes, feisty heroines, and emotion-driven happily-ever-afters. She writes what she loves to read: kink with a tender touch. Jane is a hopeless romantic who lives on the East Coast with a houseful of children and her very own Prince Charming.

What to read next? Here are some other titles by Jane you may enjoy. And don't forget to sign-up for my newsletter for a free book!

Contemporary fiction

Dark romance
   Island Captive: A Dark Romance
   Criminal by Jane Henry and Loki Renard

NYC Doms standalones

Deliverance
  Safeguard
  Conviction

Masters of Manhattan

Knave
  Hustler

The Billionaire Daddies

Beauty's Daddy: A Beauty and the Beast Adult Fairy Tale
  Mafia Daddy: A Cinderella Adult Fairy Tale
  Dungeon Daddy: A Rapunzel Adult Fairy Tale
  The Billionaire Daddies boxset

The Boston Doms
  My Dom (Boston Doms Book 1)
  His Submissive (Boston Doms Book 2)
  Her Protector (Boston Doms Book 3)
  His Babygirl (Boston Doms Book 4)
  His Lady (Boston Doms Book 5)
  Her Hero (Boston Doms Book 6)
  My Redemption (Boston Doms Book 7)

And more! Check out my Amazon author page.

You can find Jane here!
  The Club (Facebook reader group)

Website

instagram.com/janehenryauthor

bookbub.com/profile/jane-henry